Confessions Of An Abusive Man

Cover Art by Gregory Brooks

ISBN# 978-0-9818518-2-2

Published By Live Wire Publishing/ Retro Active Media Inc.

Confessions
Introduction

Dear Reader,

In an effort to make this novel interactive I created an on-line "sound track". The sound track is designed to give this novel a "movie feel," a more in-depth look into the emotions of each character. Listen to the songs that each character was listening to for a more inner active and personal connection to their feelings and personalities. There's also a message in the music; so as you read be sure to go on line and play the songs (that you will find in chronological order) at Live Wire Publishing Channel play list "Confessions Of An Abusive Man," on YouTube.com. Enjoy the full experience.

Here's some fun facts:

In every state in America, domestic violence is practiced at alarming rates. Statistically "almost half of all marriages experience at least one incident of violence. Arguably one in five marriages experience repetitive violence; defined as 5 or more violent episodes annually." Domestic abuse is generally perceived as Domestic Violence; which is not always the case. Psychological and emotional abuse is also present in relationships and marriages. When we think of Domestic Abuse generally our minds instinctively imagine a woman being abused by a man; rarely do we get an in-depth description of the male version of events.

This novel was designed to depict the "other side of the story" to provoke thought and initiate dialogue about what is going wrong in our families, homes and relationships. In hopes that we can develop a solution to some very common dysfunctional behavior patterns between men and women and ultimately inject love into our relationships and reject hate at all costs.

*Fact - While physical abuse is apparent; mental and emotional abuse is not easily detected; and in addition emotional wounds take much longer to heal and can very well last a life time.

*Fact - Wives are more than five times likely to kill their spouses than husbands; girlfriends were responsible for almost four times as many murders as boyfriends.

Fact - Domestic Violence also includes incidents in which the woman is the perpetrator and the man the victim. Heterosexual male victims receive less support and assistance than do heterosexual female victims. **– Various Sources*

Confessions Of An Abusive Man is an honest look inside many relationships behind closed doors. Both men and women have all found themselves in an abusive relationship at some point in their lives; or have possibly witnessed a friend or family member that have been in an unhealthy and abusive relationship. If you find that this book is a reflection of your love life, seek help immediately or find the strength to get out before it is too late.

***

Chapter 1

I had no idea that a woman could be so hateful, manipulative and powerful. I didn't realize that she had so much power over me. I now sit here alone wishing she was here on one hand and on the other wanting to take her head off when I see her. You see, she kidnapped the kids. It was always her threat since we've been living together but I never thought she would actually do that to me. The signs of her disrespect were evident from the beginning of our relationship. They say that the way you start a relationship is the way it will end.

The way we started has two beginnings if that makes any since to you. One when I was in prison, the other when I returned to the streets. I was loving it to be honest. I had it all; I came home to a Rider a Momi and a Shorty. She was my Shorty; I guess now you can understand why we were not going to work out. Everybody pretty much knew about each other, especially her, I told her everything. One day to challenge my stamina she told me to go fuck my rider and then come home and fuck her- see if I can handle it. I said "I'll do one better; I'll fuck both of them then come home and wear you out". I just came home from prison; all I could do is think about money and pussy. I did it and she didn't believe that I did until I called them both while she listened and they both confirmed they were worn out and I'm "a beast." That is the reason why we never worked out, I know that now. She would always be suspicious of me; I just didn't know how far she was willing to go.

I always wore nice clothes and I stayed fresh. She liked that about me. She showered like two or three times a day I only showered once maybe twice depending, but I never smelled, she said her last boyfriend feet stink. She also liked the fact that I didn't take "No shit" from anybody and I was well known for it. She said to me one day "It feels like I'm sleeping with a celebrity" I just smiled and shook my head. She was right though everybody that knew me knew I don't disrespect people and I don't tolerate being disrespected in no way, shape or form - from any one. So when she started talking crazy to me I was stung; to say the lease. What did she think? Because she was a female that she could get away with it? Or because we were fucking? It was not like she didn't know better. Why would she try me? I couldn't understand it and for a long time she got away with it because she was a girl. But I had to tell her one day "watch your mouth when you talk to me" I told her "some of the things you say to me; if you were a man I would have punched you in the face or worst" that only made her say worst things.

I never was the type to have arguments - with anybody. My reputation prevented it. Men would rather avoid a problem with me than to confront me and women admired and adored me, so verbal insults were unfamiliar territory for me. It was foreign to me and made me feel uneasy. Honestly - I was at a loss; I did not know how to deal with verbal insults. For me violence was always the solution to a conflict. Both in the streets and in prison violence solved all disputes. We had a saying "all call-outs are mandatory." So if someone disrespected you - you had to do something about it. Especially in prison... if you did not respond to a "call-out" you got labeled a punk, a herb, a pussy or a bitch. And if you got that type of label you set yourself up for being extorted, harassed, beaten or even fucked. Everybody's watching - all the time; and predators are looking for any open opportunity to come up. In prison word spreads, so that label will follow you to any prison that you go to. I spent a lot of time in prison - and everybody respected me; that should give you an inclination about how well I handled myself. I sent many men to the hospital to get stitched up... and I was molded in that way.

One can say that I was "hyper sensitive" about how anyone addressed me. And for the sake of argument; I have always been very selective with the way I addressed others. To me respect is a two-way street. I have heard a lot of people say "[people] have to earn my respect;" even her. I totally disagree. I believe that "respect is a given; but trust is earned." You suppose to respect a stranger on the street, she disagreed. It is common for New Yorkers to be rude, dismissive and disrespectful to anyone they do not know.

But in my opinion, just because you do not know someone does not mean you have a right to be disrespectful towards them. Every man, woman and child deserves respect. But not trust. That is something that develops over time.

I didn't even make borderline disrespectful jokes, because I did not want to open the door for anyone to say anything disrespectful to me; because then I would have to deal with it. And that meant certain violence. This was my defense mechanism for men; but she was not a man so I was dumbfounded. When she said things like "Your an idiot, your a jackass or you's a dumb mutherfucker." I would be shocked into silence. I would just look at her with my best SOS face (Stuck On Stupid). I had absolutely no experience at exchanging insults; so every time she verbally assaulted me it was like an electric jolt that went through my whole body. My first instinct was to strike; but my respect for women conflicted with my impulses.

I would become so angry that I would not say anything until I calmed down. (Later; it would lead me to holding in my frustration for so long that I would explode.) Once I was calm I would approach the issue as delicately as I could because I knew that she had a bad temper and anything you say can be turned into a slight to her. Just addressing her with an issue was a slight to her and because she had a bad temper and a wicked tongue, she would go off and a simple disagreement would easily turn into a shouting match, and nothing would get resolved. I tried to explain to her my experience and how it did not permit her verbal insults so she could understand how hard it was for me to tolerate it without striking out. I tried to explain why the insults had to stop; not as a means to threaten her, just so she could relate to my experiences and have some consideration about the mental rearranging that I had to go through just so I would not hit her ass. I said to her "You have to find a better way to communicate than that." She ignored that - totally. I was approaching the situation diplomatically - I was asking.

I am what is known as an Alpha Male; even though I am very soft spoken. She knew that I was an aggressive man from all that she heard about me. Maybe it was the fact that I was soft spoken and polite that threw her off, maybe she figured that if I was all that the street claim that I was; then I would more boisterous and rude to people; but that just was not my style. Plus I do not treat enemies like friends or friends like enemies; meaning she would never see my bad side because she was family. The only time she would get to see me in action is if someone tried to hurt her or disrespect her and I was present. I did not wear my gangsta hat at home. So I found myself having to remind her quite often that the way she addressed me was inappropriate.

My world was now divided into two separate realities. When I was outside around people from the hood, I was admired and praised as if I was a King. Once I crossed the threshold of her apartment I was affronted and berated as if I was a peon or a peasant. The nerve of it all made my head spin. I was always a leader - a Boss. Even at an early age I led men. I provided for them and protected them. It was easier to manage gangsters and thugs than it was to deal with her. She would try me when they would not. Murders gave me more respect than she did.

She was very abusive with her mouth. She would call me every name under the sun at this point. She called it being a "bitch" and thought it was alright. Like being a bitch to your man all day every day was cool. Just to "school" all you females that consider yourself bitches and wear it like a badge, 1 don't get mad if a man calls it like he sees it. "You get mad when I call you a bitch, but you are the first one to say that you are a bitch." It took me about two years to fix my mouth to call her a bitch, but after a while it became like her first name to me. I define a bitch as a woman that has a nasty disposition for no reason, will say something nasty to you sporadically, and it doesn't matter if they knew you for years or just met you passing by. That is a bitch to me. That's exactly what she was like.

I use to hate being in the store with her at the cash register. She used to be so nasty to the clerks and embarrass me every time for no reason. Always asking to see the manager holding up the line, and she did this for recreation because everything she was beefing over was so small that it wasn't worth the breath. One time she ran into the wrong one and I got pulled into the shit. The girl was nasty too but that's "my boo," when things get serious, there isn't no question- I'm gonna ride. I would have torn that whole supermarket up and I let that be known. In fact she had to calm me down when she probably started the shit. I truly would be more than willing; more than happy to die at battle for this woman, still to this day after all she did to me... I don't know if I'm a freak for pain or what because there was not one day she didn't say or do something to make me angry, or sad.

Still sitting in my room alone all I can think about is her and the love we made and the children we were raising together. I still try to reach out to her and settle things, but she will hear none of it. I don't really believe that we can be together after all that has happened between us. I know that I will never trust her again. It is approximately 3 months after she disappeared with the kids, jacked the rest of the money out the bank account and refuses to answer my calls. I emailed her. Not the sporadic hate-mail that she receives when a wave of anger and sadness comes over me. Just keeping in touch and telling her my thoughts like I did when we were together. I wrote:

Driving with no real direction...not knowing if I'm coming or going, just know that I am still alive...my feelings are numb...the song comes on and I roll down the windows turn up the system and hit the highway...did you hear it...could you hear me...I called to let you know that these songs told me what you did not...they also told me that everybody has problems... it bugged me out to hear how similar that Karaoke song was to my situation...but I cannot take the blame for the problems, just the part that I played in it... I'm always thinking of you... bitter or sweet...

There was a song by Lyfe Jennings called "Your done crying" that is what I was listening to at the time and it motivated that particular email.

I can't exactly put my finger on when we went wrong because we have been at each other's throats before we were married, before we had children, before we were in a "committed" relationship. She had the bad habit of telling me what to do, trying to force me to do what she wanted - when she wanted. When I did not do what she wanted she would ignore me, pretend as if I was not there or if she was really heated I became all types of names "muther fucker, asshole and idiot," was her favorite. Between direct insults and sarcasm laced with contempt; there was never a dull moment. She had an "or else" disposition that didn't work well with me from the jump street.

She knew that I was on parole so she used that as an advantage or upper hand over me in a lot of ways, like ordering me around or talking reckless to me; no matter how offensive it was. Sometimes she would indirectly put me out of her apartment in the form of reminding me that I was living in her house. The first thing I remember was when she demanded that I take her son to school because I "lived there" meaning in her apartment "Your gonna do something." That is not how you get people to want to do anything for you; that is not how you talk to people and certainly not how you talk to a regular guy; and I am not regular by anybody standards. Despite my reservations, I usually did it anyway, this probably gave her a disillusioned idea that she could put her "foot down." Now don't get it twisted I don't mind doing things for anybody especially someone I know, but some things I just don't do. Once I went against my own words and will she decided to try to pressure me to compromise all my principals and beliefs. That was too much.

Now taking her son to school don't seem like an unreasonable request does it? But keep in mind that I am not the everyday ordinary dude. I have enemies that walk the same NY streets that I walk. When we see each other, usually something jumps off. If I was with her son and something happened to him I would never be able to explain that to her. I didn't want her to find out the hard way, it was too important to play with. So there I go early in the morning creeping on the back streets so nobody that I know in the street will see me with my little step son. Then it became I had to baby sit him for her. I just came home from up north. I still was knee deep in street shit, I had no children of my own and she was only "allowing" me to parole to her house. These demands were insane to me. I don't know anything about taking care of a child; I know how to work them streets.

Still I did it- against my own will. One day she had me watching him and he went running in the street while a bunch of cars and yellow cabs were coming. Honestly that day I gave him a whuppin. I don't like spanking kids, but I had lost it; my guts were in my stomach with fear behind that shit. I think I cried after I beat him, and what I mean by "beat him" is I took his little behind home took off my belt and gave him a few licks on his behind. When she came home from work I told her that I would not watch her son again. That didn't last long either.

Chapter2

In every relationship you must know your mate. You have to understand that person and they prospective based on their experiences. You have to try to be selfless as oppose to selfish. - Sporadic thoughts

When they say that "behind every successful man - is a strong woman;" it's true. When they say "a woman can make you - or break you," that is true too. Men are influenced and inspired by women. Just a woman's presence alone can inspire a man to become a better self; or as we say in the streets "tighten his game up". Growing up in my neighborhood, I have seen broke dudes that were considered "bums" hustle hard once they got a girlfriend. They hustled so hard that some of them became the biggest drug dealers on the block. Men will do just about anything to impress his woman or make her happy. The art of suggestion is very strong.

A woman does not have to demand anything from her man, just subtly suggest things and plant a seed in a man's mind. It will flourish on its own. A women's dreams will indirectly become her man's dreams. (All she have to do is make him happy, which really does not take much more than feeding him and fucking him well.) All she would have to say is something like "I always wanted to live in a house;" and the next thing you know he is hustling hard to get her in a house. Sometimes he does not even realize that he is doing it for her, that is how powerful women can be.

When a man is emotionally invested in a woman; if her intentions are not good - he is in trouble. If he loves her; he is headed for a roller coaster ride of pain and heartache. His life can become over shadowed by that invisible dark cloud - and he can lose himself. One day you take a look in a mirror and realize - it's a stranger looking back at you.

It wasn't always bad you see, I mean when I first came home, the love we made was the bomb. It was rough, it was soft it was passionate; it was even animalistic on my behalf. I was attracted to this woman. She can be doing anything and I will get turned on. If she was doing the laundry, I wanted some. Just in from work...let's fuck...she walk by me...any reason to climb up in it. We use to tear up all the furniture she bought for her apartment having animal sex, especially that bed she had. It was a nice bed too- until I came.

I started tape recording some of our episodes, we started out fucking to hip-hop songs like the Purple Haze album, we banged out for the whole album and started up again just to see how long and how hard we were going in. We use to fuck for hours then get a sip of water and fuck some more. That was the only thing we did that was any fun though. That became the only time we got along- when we were

15

intimate. I told her that it couldn't be like that- it wouldn't last. She didn't listen to that.

First it was the invasion of my personal space. When I initially moved in it was because my aunt had kicked me out of her apartment because she claimed that me and my Rider went in her sons room, which she forbid us to do. I only had been home a week. I wasn't thinking about that damn room, in fact I wasn't even in the house all day, I only went there to wash, sleep and fuck and not exactly in that order. When my aunt said I had to leave I called Shorty to ask if I could stay- she said "yes," the next day I came with my bags. Why so fast you ask, because my aunt not only told me to get out, she called my parole officer as well. It was my first visit to his office when he asked me "What happened?" I didn't know what he was talking about, he said my aunt called and did I have a place to stay. I gave him Shorty address and he changed the paper work. He could have violated me on the spot, and I would have been right back up north one week after I was released- but he was cool.

A few weeks into staying with her my Rider moved back to her home town and I played the couch or her son's bedroom, he usually slept with her anyway. Actually he slept with her every day- in between her legs at that; I brought that to a stop though after awhile.

The first sign of disrespect was when she use to read my mail. She was always going behind me reading the mail that came for me. Mail from my Rider mostly. I knew this, but at the time I just thought it was cute so I didn't say anything. Then she started opening up my mail before I even seen it. I did not like that but I didn't say anything because I wanted to minimize the bullshit. I didn't need to be starting arguments with her and have to relocate again. Parole didn't work like that. She knew that too and I think that she took advantage of that fact. She grew worst, I stopped receiving my mail altogether.

I was very open about who I was seeing. I took it for granted that she would do the same, but she never mentioned anyone else. She would ask questions about other girls and I would answer honestly; but she did not volunteer any information; she basically kept what she was doing outside of our relationship to herself. She was still sleeping around with a guy she referred to as her "Trick" but she never told me a thing. Never mentioned one word about it on the many occasions where we discussed my sexcapades. Foolish of me to imagine that she would; I just figured that because she brought it up and I was forth coming that she would share as well - I was wrong. I was the dumb ass because I did not bother asking; but to me it was a sign of insecurity and insecurity does not look good on a man.

I don't know what made it come to mind; but one night while lying in bed after sex I asked "Are you giving mines away?" She responded "Are you giving away mines?" Which basically meant "Yeah" but she did not give me a direct answer and I did not press for a more indefinite answer; but I knew. The truth is she never gave me a direct answer about anything she was doing. Why didn't the alarms go off in my head? Was it blind love, was it the fear of being considered insecure? Why I didn't realize it until now? The truth is - she was always shady.

I don't want to risk being considered a male chauvinist; but I believe that there's a fundamental difference between men and women in regards to sexual activity. Is it old fashioned? Yes! Is it a double standard? Yes. But I don't think that a woman should be as sexually active as a man. I think that my beliefs suggest that women are more sophisticated, refined, respectable and held at a higher regard then men. Let's be honest, no male child wants to learn that his mother was like a door knob - everyone got a turn. It is the same thing for a man and his woman. No man wants a whore for his wife. Sure he will fuck a whore, slut or stripper...but he will marry the "good girl" that's just the way it is. It is not always like that, there are some exceptions, but for the most part a guy is bringing a respectable girl home to Mama. That is at least what he thinks. Women can have a dirty past and relocate, the man she meets may think that she is innocent because he doesn't know any different. But most men will not knowingly "wife" a loose female.

In my days I wanted to contribute to the house hold so I went out every day to find a job. I went to programs every day, but nobody would hire me. Jobs were scarce and even scarcer for ex-prisoners. She was the only one working and she was working hard. She worked at a bank, she was a teller. About a year into us being together I asked her in a conversation "How long have you been working at the bank?"

"6 years"

"Isn't there growth there? Like can't you get promoted?" "Yes." She had never thought of it even though she had that information in her head. "I think you should ask them how you can earn a promotion" she looked at me strangely. But the next day she came in excited "Guess what?"

"What?"

"After you said that yesterday I went in and asked my supervisor how do I get promoted, you know what she said?"

"What?"

"I was just waiting for you to ask and she made me a

manager on the spot and increased my pay...yaaaay!!!" I was happy for her and we celebrated that night.

In the beginning she agreed with me a lot. I took that to mean we shared the same or similar beliefs. She was not argumentative either, controlling at times yes, but confrontational - no. After while all that changed. Her true self came out and stayed. I thought it was a passing phase, a mood swing, a PMS thing; but it was not. Now I wish I could have got a warning; like the ones they show on TV from the American Broadcast System "WARNING! This is NOT a test...This is the real thing! Exit your homes immediately, get to the nearest bomb shelter in your area. We repeat - This Is Not A Test....Booooop!" This way I could have run for cover. But like a silly rabbit; I fell for the old karat on the string trick.

It's like the girl you meet that looks beautiful. Long eye lashes, long hair, drop dead gorgeous smile, smells really good all the time. Always looks nice and presentable. When you go over to her place, it is always immaculate. Then when you get to know her - it was all a mirage. All the pleasantries come to a complete halt. All of a sudden she no longer gets dressed up for you, she walks around with that "morning look" - busted. She only gets dressed up for others, special occasions, when you'll going out or someone is visiting. You are no longer important enough for her to dress up for. Her place is no longer immaculate; looks like a hurricane done blown through there.

The bitter truth is - it all was fake. Fake hair, fake eye lashes, fake nails...make-up - everything about her was fake. Not only her looks; but her mannerisms as well. Now she's burping and farting around you without saying "excuse me," you didn't even know that she farted before. First she was nice and sweet, attentive and agreeable - not any more. She did that just to lure you in. Once she feels that she "has" you - she becomes the wicked witch. It's like she is possessed with some type of evil spirit. You know what happened? You have been scammed by a girl. Like Malcolm X would say "You've been had, conned, hood winked - bamboozled." But your male ego cannot accept the fact that you've been played by a girl. So you stick around and find yourself overlooking things that you know is unacceptable. You start asking yourself dumb ass questions like "What happened to the pretty girl? Is this the same woman I met?" And you find yourself acting like a "crack-head", chasing that first high that will never come back, no matter how much cocaine you smoke.

But you cannot get around the simplest questions like why women go through all the trouble of pretending to be something that they are really not? Is it because they know that no one in his right mind would sign up for that? And once you're trapped; what do you do then? Fight like hell to gain control of the situation or fight your way out.

One night while walking in the Bronx I saw these three girls walking in the projects, they were singing at the top of their lungs "Let me cater to you," by Destany Child. It made me think of Shorty. I didn't acknowledge it then but I was developing feelings for her.

When she came home, every day she came home, I would have the apartment clean from top to bottom. I am good at cleaning; she said I clean "better than women," whatever that means. I usually worked really hard and fast, not to just impress her but to make sure she didn't have to do anything but take care of me and her son, than go to sleep. I would even have a foot bath for her and a hot tub ready when she stepped through the door.

I would give her a pedicure then make love to her all night. She always had problems getting up for work, I mean we would be getting it in until the sun peeped over the clouds. That was a good day for me. I didn't know it then but I was falling.

She had two phones. One house phone and a cell phone. When my cell phone was disconnected, she would let me borrow hers especially when I had a job possibility, or if I was going to report to parole. She had a lot of male friends. Over 20 in her cell and just about 8 guys calling the house, 3 regularly. I was cordial with all of them. I'm sure they didn't know at first that we were even intimate with each other because I was so polite to them. If she wasn't there I would tell them to "call back later" and I would tell her that they called. I even took down names sometimes. Then her baby father called.

"Put that bitch on the phone" he says to me when I answered. I thought "No hello or nothing huh?" What I said to him was "You don't have to talk like that, I put her on the phone whenever someone calls, that is not necessary." I knew that he knew that I was messing with her because he use to read the mail that I sent to her when I was up north. She told me that he use to beat her ass because of the letters I sent. "Nigga did you hear me? I said put that bitch on the phone."

"What?" Click. I banged the phone on him. He immediately called back, I picked up just as polite as I did before. "Hello???"

"Nigga did you hang up the phone on me?"

"Listen you don't have to talk like that."

"Don't tell me how to talk, that's my kid in there."

"I never said that you couldn't speak to your kid." It went on and on and got more heated until he invited me to meet him outside. I was shocked. I know that he knew about my

23

reputation on the streets. Didn't he know that I would do him filthy? I immediately thought he was packing. I didn't accept the invitation, but I made the decision then that he would get dealt with the next time I laid eyes on him. That is what made me relocate to Momi house. I could not afford to get violated by parole over this dumb nigga. So I went to the Momi.

Momi was the kind of chic that we like to call a "Ride Or Die" in the hood. She knew how to treat her man and she knew the streets. When I first got home; she called my cell; and I didn't even know how she got my number. When I answered she said "Nigga you been home all this time and didn't holla at me!" I was only home for 5 days. She said "Where you at?"

"I'm in the Bronx... 161st street."

"Wait right there. Don't go nowhere nigga!"

I smiled "Aight."

She drove up in her SUV approximately 15 minutes later and said "Get in." I did, she was happy to see me. "Nigga what you wearing?" I was "Fresh;" at least I thought so. Everything I had on was brand new. She said "Get dressed." I was clueless. "Your clothes is in the back. Climb back there and get dressed." I did. And sure nuff, there were boxes filled with Polo everything. She yelled from the driver's seat

"Take all that bullshit off and get dressed... its draws and sox in there too. I'm taking you to get some sneakers; what size do you wear?" That's how Momi was; and I love her to this day because of it.

Shorty would call Momi house in the middle of the night; I mean after midnight while me and Momi was asleep; to give me "messages," that people left for me on her answering machine. She could have called at a decent hour; but Momi didn't stress it so neither did I. As much as I loved Momi and enjoyed her company; we had other issues that made it impossible to be together. For one, she was basically running for president. Her apartment was like Grand Central Station. Not only that; she had a history with a "friend" of mine.

That was a somewhat uncomfortable situation for me because she was the baby mother to an old friend that I considered a brother when we were growing up. Him and I weren't exactly on good terms at the time, but that didn't make it any easier to be with a girl that he actually had a baby with.

That was kind of crossing the line for me, but he was a habitual "line crosser" himself and I was in a bad position- so I went for it. But when I woke up to her in the mornings I felt a pang of guilt to see his son running around, so I knew that my conscience would not allow it to work out. I have one of them damn nagging ass consciences that forces me to do the right thing, maybe its God but whenever I know something is wrong I absolutely *have* to make it right. Either that or I will subconsciously sabotage a situation, and life itself will straighten things out.

We were better friends than anything. She was the type of person that I could talk to about anything. She was down for whatever and she was sharp as fuck. She thought like a man, but was lady like. That was butter. If she had chosen another baby father, we would have been perfect together. I kept telling myself "better to keep it as friends because that last longer" but I ignored this thought and just went with the flow. I wanted to get my parole transferred to Manhattan anyway because that's where I was most of the time. I only went to the Bronx to rest even when I was living with Shorty.

It was going good back with Momi but one night Shorty crept into my mind. It was the music. While Momi was more like me Shorty was the opposite. I listened to hip-hop she listened to R&B, even though sometimes it was irritating, it was a balance I guess. Momi listened to hip-hop too and that made me long for that sensuousness that I got around Shorty. There was one song that Momi loved and it was by Usher "Your gonna want me back" she loved it so much that she bought us tickets to the Usher concert in Madison Square Garden. I enjoyed myself, but when she took me to the Jay-Z concert; that was one of the most enjoyable times I had in my life. When I was in prison watching music videos a Jay-Z song came on called "Encore" it was a concert recording... It looked like they were having a party in the arena. I whispered to myself, "One day I'm going to be there." And Momi made that day come true.

One day I gave Shorty a ring. I can't remember how long I had been living with Momi but I called and she answered. I told her I want to see her she said "come over." That night we had sex. It wasn't all that- we had better, but we did it. She left passion marks all over my neck and I let her, so when Momi flipped and asked me to leave, I didn't put up much of a protest. I moved back in with Shorty.

One day a month or two after we split I called Momi and left a message on her phone, I didn't speak I put my MP3 head phones to the receiver, I was listening to "Superstar" by Usher and every time I heard a song from that "Confessions" album, I thought of her.

***

Now I'm looking at Shorty a little different. I just go with the flow of life, I try not to dictate my moves, I go with God, where ever he leads me. But one day I remember looking at her and telling myself "Yeah, I could fuck her for the rest of my life." And that really meant in my heart that I loved her, and she was attractive to me. I ignored the "I love her" part though and I never told her how I felt. I know now that women need to be told, but I've always believed that "actions speak louder than words." I've learned that that does not work in relationships with a woman; but it's too late for that now.

We use to take sporadic walks in the beginning and I would just keep walking with no specific destination in mind. I think we went to Popeye's that night, but while walking I was moved to recite a Nas song for her called "Black Girl Lost." I thought that she would be impressed by the lyrics and it would provoke some sort of dialogue about Black women; but it did not and we walked back home in virtual silence.

I still had a lot of lust in me though. I expected to have two or three women at a time, like they do in them "pussy books" I got off to in prison. I was more handsome then them dudes in my opinion, so I just knew it would be easy for me. I was shy though, that was an advantage that she never knew that she had over our relationship. I don't approach women. There's only a hand full of times that I drummed up the courage to approach a woman that I liked. I don't know why I was like that, I knew that I wasn't hard on the eyes, I just felt uncomfortable doing it. Maybe I feared rejection, I don't know, but what I do know is most of the women I have slept with approached me. She was one of them, she should have known.

If she knew that about me she would have never been stressing over it later in life and punishing me for things that I was not doing. See she has a wild imagination that she forces upon me. I'll explain that later.

To her defense, I was flirtatious with some women. To my defense, she started the flirtation around other men and pretended she was doing nothing. She has done worst things in my opinion on the issue of flirting. I could be flirtatious but what did she really expect from a dude that spent the majority of his years in some type of jail or prison? What she took as an excuse was my reality. She never lived in a cell for a whole day. Let alone do a total of 15 years inside some cell. I did. I knew what it was like to be sexually deprived. I wasn't gay so the only thing for me was a kiss on a visit. When she was "exploring" her sexuality all those years, I was exploring my hand. She couldn't understand this and didn't even want to hear it. I tried to talk about it to get it out my system but she closed the door for communicating on it totally.

Chapter 3

The biggest problem that I had with her jealousy over my flirtation was the fact that she was very flirtatious herself, to the point of disrespect. She pretends that she is not doing anything and she stick to her story too. She wrote me one day when I was up north and told me her baby father had beat her ass because some niggas on the street tried to holla at her when she was walking with him. She said he wasn't a man because he should have stepped to them. I agreed with her. She told me that he always beat her ass; he even beat her for writing me while I was in prison. See at that time she was supposed to be "my girl" it was all her idea. What I didn't know is while she had the title of "my girl" it was only for my information because I found out later that she was trying to "Do the family thing" with him because she had a son with him.

I wondered why I couldn't get any mail from "my girl" I got more mail from my friend and my Rider but I was claiming her and they knew it. I found out she was "doing the family thing" when I came home. She never informed me and she only had been to see me twice in the 6 years that I did up there, once of which I had paid for from inside prison. That is why I came home to my Rider instead of her, because she didn't do the bid. That's another story. Back to her baby's father- that is why I never liked the nigga from the jump because I use to hear all these stories about him beating her ass. I wanted to fight him a long time ago before she was a thought on the relationship side. I knew of the abuse because her brother and I were tight and grew up together. I heard those stories for years.

Her flirtation was like this, if we were walking down the street together and some guy looks at her to check her out, she will hold his stare right in front of me. I picked it up quick and that's when I stopped walking beside her. I would walk behind her from that point on. That could cause a fight. If she staring in another man's face, to him that means she either isn't in a relationship with the nigga beside her or she don't give a fuck. That is an invitation. If the nigga thinks he's thorough or a gangsta; then he may say something, then I have to chin check him or worst depending on the severity of the situation. To prevent a bad decision, I just stopped walking with her. I didn't say anything to her about it, why would I? She would just deny it anyway so I dealt with it like that. That is probably why ol' boy slapped her up I reasoned later.

Before she made that dummy move I use to hold her hand every now and then in the streets. I wasn't into it though because I was always "on point" walking the streets. I never wanted to get caught slipping, that was another reason why it suited me just fine walking behind her. Because nobody would know I was with her. This way if I was attacked or had to attack someone, she could get away unharmed without getting pulled into a war that extended from my troubled past. That worked out to my advantage later.

The other flirtation I seen in her was when my cousin or my friend came over to the house. She would do some shit like go take a shower while they were there. In that small ass two bedroom apartment. She couldn't wait until my company left; she had to come out the shower with only a towel on dripping from head to toe and run to the bedroom as if she was invisible or something.

It was embarrassing and she pretended like she was doing nothing wrong. I didn't bring that up on the spot either, I ignored it just to avoid problems but eventually I did mention it when she started coming at me for being on the phone with my friends. Male or female it didn't matter, but she made her presence known when I was on the phone with my female friends. She went as far as cursing me out when I was on the phone. That was our very first argument.

One day while on I was on the house phone with my friend, her girlfriend called. When I clicked over her friend was being rude and demanding me to put her on the phone "Now!" and how I'm just a "Fucking visitor" in that house, yada yada ya. I didn't know where that came from and I just clicked back over to continue my conversation. She called Shorty cell phone immediately; I could hear her talking and knew it was coming, I thought she would wait to address it later that night but not 10 seconds later Shorty burst in the room yelling, screaming and cursing at me for hanging up the phone on her friend. She had her friend listening on the other end cause she still had the cell phone on in her hand and my friend listening on my end. I was so embarrassed that she almost got smacked that day. I hung up the phone with my friend and barked on her. Thinking back now, I believe that she convinced her friend to call so she could create some chaos and cause a problem between me and my lady friend.

What she didn't know at that point was her friend tried to fuck me and was mad that I didn't give her any rhythm. It was one hot summer day, I remember I was feeling really good and was on my way out the door when the phone rang. Shorty was in the shower so I answered, it was her "best friend", I said "Hello?"

"Is this Him?"

"Yeah."

"Why we never fucked?" she asked. I looked at the phone in disbelief. Now I know that Shorty told her we were fucking already, I didn't know if that was a set up or what- I banged on the bath room door and handed the phone to Shorty. I didn't even respond to that bullshit. I didn't tell

Shorty either, I forgot about it as soon as it happened, but it would come up later.

That was not the only time this particular "friend" came at me. One day she came over the apartment while me and my Homie was leaving, she got in the elevator with us. She said to my Homie "He's scared of me" my Homie laughed and said "Nah, what she talkin' about bro?"

"I don't know what she's talking about." I said and made a nervous chuckle.

"I threw the pussy at him, he scared of pussy."

"Wooooow! Say it ain't so Homie!" We all laughed but I know that she was serious. She was cute...fuckable even; but I did not want to disrespect Shorty like that. I fucked one of my main girl's best friends when I was younger and things just got messy. I did not want to do that to Shorty.

We disagreed about almost everything; but I learned that simple disagreements turned into heated arguments with her. I made it a point not to send her to work angry. Whatever it was we were arguing over; I put it behind me and made it my business to make up with her. If we both fell asleep before I an issue was resolved, I would wake up in the middle of the night - and down came the panties. One night I failed to wake up and she was already fresh out of the shower, putting on her make-up when I walked in the bathroom; got behind her and fucked her brains out over the bathroom sink. I did not send her into the world angry with me. I did it because my girl was fly, and I wanted to keep her eyes on the prize - me. I did not want some other guy doing what I was supposed to be doing at home. I took special interest in keeping her satisfied. I knew that dissatisfied women were more receptive to another man's advances, especially when they were angry. Some women would fuck another man just out of spite, and I wanted to prevent that from happening.

The second thing that I noticed was when we were alone she always had a bad attitude, but when someone came over her attitude would immediately change. She would be so nice to people, and it bugged me out. I couldn't believe how quick she could flip the script. When my cousin or friend would come over, she would be extra nice and always walking in the kitchen past us. She would offer them a plate of food before me, served them before me and when she ran out of something she would say so in front of them and laugh. This is no way to treat her "King". Being a good host is respectable, but you always take care of home first. I didn't like that, but I let it ride.

For some reason I end up going to her "best friend" apartment. I was there to pick up something; I just can't remember what. Her friend was trying to make small talk with me; but I wanted to get out of there as soon as possible. It was a long train ride back home. Her friend kept bending over so I could see her ass; then she would look over her shoulder to see if I was watching. No disrespect; but she was hideous. She looked a hot mess, hair wrapped in a dirty old scarf, dirty old t-shirt with stains on it, extra tight jeans that look like she been in them for a few days. And here she was trying to flirt with me; I was dying laughing inside. Back in the days she had a nice figure. Her ass was fat... I think she still thought she had it; but the glory days were over baby. Her stomach hung over her jeans and stuck out the bottom of her t-shirt - hideous.

Her other friend didn't look so bad; but she was overweight too. Then it was her aunt. One day we went uptown together to pick up her son. Her aunt came just as we were leaving. It was my first time meeting her. She said "So this is the famous one I've been hearing about!" I smiled and greeted her with a respectful "Nice to meet you." She said "What you got?" I did not understand the question. "Huh?" She was looking dead at my crotch; then looked up at me with a smirk on her lips "What you got that's making my niece go crazy?" I could not believe her boldness. My mouth was open but no words came out; Shorty had just went inside to get her son while I waited outside for her. I looked back to see if she was coming to save me. Her aunt continued "You don't have to be shy; I'm grown, I know what's going on." I started "dying laughing" and asked myself "Is she saucy or something?" She laughed then touched my chest. Shorty came out - just in time, we said good bye and left. As I walked down the street; I was shocked. I didn't know what to think of that... her aunt was not bad looking; but really?!

Bills were coming in but I paid for none of them. She was the only one working. To my defense I was out there every day all day trying, but how did she know that? As far as she knew I was kicking my feet up. But I am not of that pedigree. She still needed help and I felt worthless in a way because I was not producing the results we needed. I was not contributing and it bothered me. Eventually I said that I would go get some food stamps so we can have some food in the house. Honestly I don't recall who brought it up first but I did it. I have a serious complex about things like that. I made thousands of dollars on the street, so to be in the welfare office was a serious blow to my male ego. Not to mention my reputation. As much as I didn't want to be seen in there I sure nuff was spotted anyway.

I got the food stamps, gave her the card and she started to cook more. She use to eat out every day. The corner store McDonalds or the Chinese restaurant across the street. Every now and then the Kuchefretos. I wanted her to cook more because I thought it was a waste of money. Who was I to say anything about money though when I wasn't paying the bills? She wouldn't say it direct or in an argument; she would just complain every now and again "I wanted to get a new phone, but I can't because I gotta pay all the bills." She thought she was catering to my male ego, by not directly asking me or saying that I was not making money. But what she did not do directly she did indirect; like when she reminded me that she gave up her "trick" when she started "fucking with" me.

He had a girl but he would fuck her on the side, take her places and buy her things. Pay a bill every now and then. Drive her around and shit like that, he had an income I don't know what he did and didn't ask. She would even ask me to watch her son while she went out with him when I first came home.

When she broke down her whole relationship with him I had respect for their friendship and didn't expect her nor ask her to break ties with him. I did not consider him a threat in the least. I told her "He is a real friend, hold on to that, real friends are rare" she gave me a look that I took for surprise and respect.

I always had trust issues in regards to females; not because of insecurities but because of experience. I like to think that I'm a good judge of character; but now days I have to question my own judgment. Why the trust issues? Well, back in the days when I was hustling in my old neighborhood, I was walking pass my old building when this woman called me out of her window. When I looked up she asked "Can you get me a White Owl from the store?" A White Owl is a cigar we used to roll our weed in at the time. At first we used Phillie Blunts, then White Owls, then Dutch Masters. Now they smoke weed in Blunt Wraps. But anyway, I already had a few for myself so I said "I'm coming up!"

When I got in she tossed about 5 or 6 nickel bags on the table; although I only smoked dimes or 20's of chocolate, I decided to smoke with her anyway. She was mad cool. To me she was grown. She had to be at least 28 years old at the time; I was only 16. But I was well known in my hood... I had a "rep" and mostly everybody knew me or heard of me - young and old.

I rolled up a blunt while she busied herself tidying up her apartment. When I sparked it; I called for her, I said "Come hit this" as I exhaled a mouth full of smoke. She came and sat beside me and said "Smoke" meaning 'keep smoking'. At the same time she unbuckled my pants and began to suck my dick. I must admit - I was surprised. I kept smoking, laid my head back and enjoyed the festivities. I bust in her mouth and she jumped up, grabbed her mouth and ran in the kitchen. "Why you cum in my mouth?" I smiled.

"It felt so good; I couldn't help it...here smoke" I passed her the blunt.

"Put that thing away" she said. I did and rolled up another bag of smoke.

Moments later there were keys turning the lock - her man came home from work. He was a Jamaican dude. A respectable dude as far as I could tell; but I didn't know him personally. When he saw me sitting on the couch, smoking next to his baby's mother, his face flashed a strand of irritation. He greeted me "Whats up?" I greeted him with the same "Whats up?" and then he walked straight to the back where the bedrooms were and called her. They were arguing.

I could barely make out what he was saying but I could hear her loud and clear "Muthafucka don't be telling me what to do in my muthafucken house! Muthafucka where's my money? You still ain't gave me shit for the rent and its due next week. You said you were gonna give me money for my hair and nails two weeks ago! You ain't give me shit. Don't start coming in here tryin' to tell me what the fuck I should be doing!" I'm thinking "He's about to slap fire out of her" but they came back in the living room. I said "I'm out." She said "You don't have to leave." Then he chimed in "Everything is crisp Dada... Just cool." I said "Nah, I got to go get this money." I looked at her "You good?" I asked. She said "Yea." That was enough for me; I tore ass.

I thought it over and felt bad for dude; even though I didn't know him. Here he was working a 9 to 5 everyday, selling weed (to make extra funds) and sponsoring her habit, paying bills, giving her money for herself, providing for his child; and while he's at work she's sucking my dick and got me smoking his weed. That is the ultimate disrespect. If she did that with me on some spare of the moment type shit; it don't take a rocket scientist to figure out that she did it to other dudes as well. For reasons like that, I did not trust females. Not only was she sleeping with other dudes behind his back, but she had the nerve to curse him out right in front of me. With the same mouth that was filled with cum moments ago. Some females have no boundaries - everything goes.

She was not the only one. I was "Jody" in many situations. I fucked a lot of other dudes women; and these dudes loved and trusted their girlfriends. That's when I started wearing those t-shirts that said "Bitches ain't shit but Hoes and Tricks." I had them in several different colors...and believe it or not - those shirts got me pussy too. A girl would see me on the street and say "That's disrespectful" then the next thing you know she's giving me her number.

The way I would describe a female like this: There's 3 different levels and 5 different categories to a female. First there's the girl; she is immature and curious about the

Amiri

world and wants to experience new things. Her curiosity and innocents accompany irrational levels of trust. That makes her easy to swindle, mislead and deceive. Then there's the lady, she is respectable, decent, self-conscious and particular about what she wants. She is eager to explore her sexual impulses, but only when she is comfortable with the right person. She is discovering her own identity but she has a firm conviction about what she will or will not do. Then there's the woman. A woman is a lady of grace. She has reached a higher level of maturity and is molded in her ways. She is experienced, decisive, self-assured and comfortable in her own skin - she knows herself. With all the personality traits of a lady, but in addition; she is responsible. Every lady or woman still has that little girl inside.

Then there's the Bitches and the Hoes. The Bitches, they are confrontational and love to argue. They feel alive when they are creating chaos or problems, they can have some of the qualities of a lady, but their mannerisms, language, attitude and desire for attention makes them immature. The Hoes are thrill seekers. They have little respect for anything or anyone outside of their own interest. They use their bodies to fulfill their needs or desires and find pleasure knowing that they are wanted sexually regardless of how short lived it may be.

Finally I landed a security guard position. I was happy to be working but it didn't pay shit and I don't talk to the police so I would never be able to do my job effectively. But it was sweet when I landed in Grand Concourse Village.

I use to smoke my trees outside then go in my booth and talk to Shorty all night. I did that shit every day for months, Shorty use to complain that she always was sleeping on her feet at work for talking to me all night. One night I called and she sounded timid. I was like "What's up?"

She said "Guess who here."

"Who?"

"Your friend."

"Who Homie? What the fuck he doing in my house?" I said in a joking manner. "He just came over, he said he thought you were here."

"I hear that shit." I said meaning he knows I work the night shift. I continue "How long he been there?"

"About 15 minutes."

"For what?"

"Oh he said he was cold, it's a storm outside so I made him some hot tea."

43

"What??? Put that nigga on the phone."

"Hello?"

"Nigga what you doing in my house?"

"Hahahaha...no I thought you was here, just came from the block and I was coming to check you before I went uptown." "Nigga you know I be working at night."

"Yeah but I forgot my dude."

"Got yo ass drinking tea in my house and shit." I laughed, he did too. I said "Okay put Shorty on the phone."

"Hello?"

"Aight, I'll call you back in a minute."

"Alright." I called back 30 minutes later and immediately started my conversation "Its mad cold out here. I'm in this bullshit booth in the middle of everything, but I'm gonna smoke my shit anyway."

"Yeah if it's cold you should stay inside."

"I am I just go out there to smoke."

"Um we still talking."

"What you mean by that?" I thought she was going to say she was talking with her friend on the other end, I was going to tell her "this my time" but she said "I'm still talking to your homeboy."

"He still there??? Why he still there?"

"Cause we talking." Sounded like she wanted to continue her conversation to me so I said "Okay, I'll call back."

"Okay."

I called back 45 minutes later, "What's good?"

"He still here"

"Word, okay." She called me about an hour later. I started the conversation like nothing ever happened. I was a little irritated because she fucked up my routine. I was bored in that damn booth. Then she said "I'm mad at you." That is what pissed me off. "Mad at me, for what?"

"Nothing."

"No you don't just say something then say forget it- how you mad at me?"

"Cause your friend."

"What you mean?" It took her another hour of me probing for her to tell me that they were "talking about sex". I was not surprised knowing my Homie, but I was disappointed that she didn't kick his ass out from the jump street. She said that she didn't say nothing much she just listened while he told her "What he do and what he likes." She did not get into detail. I was only covering my anger and ignoring my grown ass rational, I should have left her then.

Instead I went to Homie house the next morning to check him. Truth is that when we were younger we use to share girls; I never was into sharing a girl that I was living with or took seriously though. Plus we were grown now so those childish games were a part of the past. Unless I gave him the green light he had no business trying to push up on mine. I told him that he violated, he looked at the ground the whole time. His Wifey was in the next room so I left it alone so she wouldn't hear us talking about that.

I move on and put that out of my mind too. The drama continued, one day I heard her talking to her friend about putting me "the fuck out" because I didn't want to babysit her son. She did this right in front of me but she thought I didn't know because she spoke to her friend in "God body" alphabet. It was like another language or means of communication for the Nation Of Gods and Earths. For some reason she just imagined I didn't know it. I was actually surprised that she knew it but I never said anything about it. She spoke about another man in front of me one day but I didn't say anything because I wanted to hear what she had to say, how far she would go- she had no boundaries. She made jokes about me with her friend, and they laughed at me right in my face. On this particular day I revealed to her that I knew it. She spelled out "drama" and I said it out loud. She started yelling, laughing and telling her friend that I knew it all that time. Why didn't I tell her? She felt like an ass, but she never apologized. To this day she never apologized for anything that she did.

Instead she would pretend that she did nothing. She would start an argument out the clear blue sky; for something minor. She would start yelling at me like I was a child (something she knew I hated) and once I got ready to explode - she would turn it all around on me. She would say things like "Why you mad?" as if she had no idea. I began to believe that she was bipolar.

At first I was impressed that she knew God Body lessons; I had a false impression that she had "knowledge of self" and cared about education, elevation and culture - I was terribly mistaken. It did not reflect in the way she carried herself nor how she expressed herself. Thinking back now; I suppose the only reason why she studied the Nation of The Gods and Earths was because her boyfriend at the time was into it and she probably was just trying to be down or trying to impress him. Clearly she did not study for the right reasons; because once their relationship came to an end; she stopped following the culture, stopped attending the meetings, stopped studying the lessons, she even started eating pork.

I am not a member of the Nation of the Gods and Earths; but I have studied lessons myself. One thing that I took from my experience was it is very important to know your history as well as your present conditions. Even though it was rarely a time when she was behaving like one; I told her that she was a beautiful Black Queen.

I tried to educate her about how and why Black Families were systematically destroyed. I even apologized for the generations of my forefathers' inability to protect our Black women. I promised that I would die before I allowed someone to hurt her. I told her because of slavery Black women were bitter with the Black male; and I understood why. At that time Black women had no reason to respect a Black man as he was forced to watch his woman be raped and abused in the hands of wicked White males.

I informed her about how the welfare system was used as a tool to undermine the development of Black manhood and pit the woman against the man. I educated her about how the system was designed to reverse the roles and make women the head of the household; to stagnate Black male leadership roles in the family unit and community. How Black men were systematically denied work, but Black women were given jobs. This made the Black woman the provider, which reversed the roles at a crucial time for Black males, as they were trying to define and exercise manhood. It frustrated Black men and attacked his self-esteem; which made him bitter against the world and even the success of his woman. With the lack of education and communication skills; he could not describe effectively that it was a system designed to disrupt Black families; if he even realized it himself. He was constantly under the impression (whether real or imagined) that his woman was screwing around with her White bosses.

The woman was constantly being fed the lies that "Black men are lazy, they don't want to work" and she was beginning to believe it, after all - she had a job. He became the enemy in his own home, perceived through eyes of pity and disgust by his wife and children; he began to self-medicate as a means to escape. Alcohol and drugs numbed his feelings and made him abusive. Eventually his heart became bitter and cold against women and he became a rolling stone, a gigolo - a pimp. This was the evolution of destruction of Black Families from one generation to another. I said we have to break the chain. I believe that she must have been singing "Fa la la la la la" in her head whenever I spoke or attempted to enlighten her, because she never tried to apply anything I attempted to teach her. And when I asked do she remember discussing these issues or subjects she will say "I don't know what your talking about." All I could do is shake my head and say "Forget it."

She had no memory loss when she was entertaining the bullshit or when recollecting an argument. Tragic.

Chapter 4

I listened to Jay-Z a lot and Shorty liked this one particular song that she identified with our relationship it was called "Soon you'll understand."

Now we at a point that none of her friends like me cause she's always on the phone talking dirty about me. I didn't care they didn't know me and I don't fuck with none of them like that anyway. She did the same thing with her family; but one day while I was taking a bath her aunt called. I answered and we got into an extensive conversation. Shorty was in the bathroom listening to the discussion because I had the phone on speaker. I didn't care that she listened because I told her everything that I was discussing with her aunt; it was nothing new. But her aunt said something that shocked us both. I already knew because I was living the experience, but when her aunt blurted out "I know that she is not no angel; she takes people for granted, she's a selfish, nasty little bitch. I have been putting up with her shit for years..." When I looked at Shorty face; I could tell that she was shocked and hurt. I felt sorry for her; apparently, she didn't know her aunt felt that way about her. But she has a way of affecting people like that.

I understood that she was hurt and that is not a good way to find out how your family members feel about you. But the question is why? Why did her aunt feel this way? Why would she say a thing like that to a non-family member? Instead of evaluating why her aunt was so frustrated with her; she decided there and then that her aunt was "Not to be fucked with anymore" (note: she did still use her aunts babysitting services when she needed her though). Still I took the phone off speaker and ended the call so I could lick her wounds. The bad thing is, her aunt did not know that Shorty was listening; that's probably why she felt comfortable being real with me. I silently wished that I would have told her that I had her on speaker or took her off speaker altogether. I wanted assistance in fixing the problems with Shorty, not creating more. I cherish family and I did not want her to be at odds with her aunt or vice versa; but I also didn't want her aunt to have a one sided story that made me out to be the villain.

I'm doing everything I can do to try to get paid. I started making shirts and selling them on the street. I was so hungry I took a shopping cart and hit the streets. I went to my block with that damn shopping cart. I use to have workers on that block I could hear niggaz in the back of my mind mocking me "damn homie/ in 94 you were the man homie, what the fuck happened to you?" I didn't even care. I was not going back to jail for nothing. They could have that block, all the fake gangstas, old and new hustlers, all the rats and roaches and all the police. I was done with that.

I didn't make a bunch of gwop selling shirts either so I

maintained a job in Brooklyn. That was a good job for me; it was an Old Italian guy that was cool as fuck. All he wanted to do was building maintenance on the building he owned and art work. He really just paid me to hang out with him. I grew to love this man. When I use to have problems with Shorty I confided in him and he gave me advice.

She had a narcissistic attitude. She felt as long as she had a job, people were expendable, even her friends and family. She was more concerned about her own happiness than being responsible; especially when it came to others - even her own mom. I don't like hospitals; I have a mild phobia when it comes to hospitals. That is one of the reasons why I was in so much pain. When my mother died, I had left her on her death bed. I was a teenager, seeing my mother deteriorate and die right in front of me was too much for my young heart and selfish mind to bear - so I ran. It was the dark cloud haunting me in my adult years. I wish I had stayed by my mom's side; at the foot of her bed so when she transcended back to the essence, she would know that I was there. I shared that experience with her because her mother was in the hospital and when we visited her, her mom would beg her to take her home.

One day I had to leave the room before they seen me cry; I felt so bad for her. Mama Love tried to negotiate with her daughter saying that she would get a "live-in" nurse; but

Shorty would not even listen. It was not even Shorty's apartment; it really was her mothers, Shorty just took it over when Mama Love got sick. I shared my story and tried to reason with her on her mothers behalf, but she would hear none of it. I left it alone; thinking that it was too hard for her to deal with emotionally; but at the end of the day it was selfish. I said "let your mother come home" she said that she "could not care for her" and did not want to discuss it. So I did not want to visit her mom in the hospital; because I wanted her out of there. I guess it was my way of trying to make up for not being there with my mother; but Shorty made me feel like it was none of my business. I put the discussion off for another day; but if I was thinking clearly I would have realized her dismissive character. If it was too painful or uncomfortable for her; she would have nothing to do with it and dismiss it altogether, even family.

She was quick to write people off if someone did not do what she wanted. If her friend or aunt could not watch her son, she would talk about them like a dog, "Fuck that bitch; I don't need her anyway; she grimey. She a crack head, she a bum, they will need me before I need them, fuck em. She don't pay my bills, she ain't fucking me; so fuck her." I would just listen to allow her to let off steam, but at the end of the day - she really felt that way. She really treated people like that. She would call when she needed something; other than that you were a non-issue. Her money was her God. That came first, before anything or anyone else. Her job is what gave her security; as long as she had a job and could pay her bills; then she can talk any kind of way to anybody and discard people like a worthless peice of chewing gum that you may find on the ground or underneath an elementary school desk. Don't get me wrong; we all need money to survive, but it was more than money for her; it was a false power of independence, she believed that since she was "independent" and "grown" she can treat people anyway she wanted which was usually badly.

She didn't even make that much money, and with her attitude she could get fired at any given moment. She stayed having problems with her supervisors at work, so I didn't see why she felt so "secure." The people you shit on will be the same ones you will have to crawl back to and beg for help. I tried to snap her out of that type of "stinking thinking" - but to no avail. Once she made up her mind about something - nothing could persuade or convince her otherwise.

Reflecting

Our second really big argument was over watching her son. I had planned to go to the Poconos with my friend and on the day I was to go she said I "had" to watch her son because she had to work and nobody else could watch him. And I'm "there" meaning living with her so "who else supposed to do it?" I end up watching her son. I didn't get to go to the Poconos.

It was a regular day and I was in the mood to build with Shorty. I took out a business plan that I designed while I was up north and I wanted her to take it on. It was for a unisex solon. I had created a very detailed business plan for the business. It was complete with architectural outlines of a 3 story building, services that it would provide and five to ten year projections. I thought she could do it. I knew she could do it because we are capable of doing anything we put our minds to. I wrote 3 business plans in prison; I would work on one, she could work on the other - I told her. I wanted to upgrade her. Shape and mold her into a beautiful Black business woman. I told her that she could have the idea, and the plan. I just wanted her to be encouraged to do something. I needed a woman that had the same kind of drive, determination and goal orientation to match my own, so when we came home from a long day of work, we will both have something to share and enhance our lifestyle. I believed that she may have accomplished more and faster than myself because she's a woman, but she had this blank look on her face when I asked "So what you think?" She listened but she couldn't phantom having her own business. That was the end of that conversation.

I was designing some new fashion designs when the phone rang. I answered like I always did. "Hello?" "Put that bitch on the phone" "oh you still on that shit?" click. When he called right back I yelled for her to answer the phone. I could tell that they were arguing. I ignored it. I stayed in my lane and continued to design, that is until 30 minutes later when there was a knock on the door. I said to myself "I know this nigga didn't come to this house- I'm not that lucky." See I was prepared for anything at this point. I went to the peep hole and low and behold- there he was. I immediately answered, when I did that tuff tony shit went right out the window. He stood there still, cowering and begging her "that bitch" to do something. He said "you not gonna let him do this Shorty" I said "don't call her now, let's go." He got in the elevator with me; he was really edgy, like he wanted to just grab me. I read his thoughts and told him "don't do it"

He didn't come to handle business, I realized that now. So I told him that he violated and we had to fight. I respect a fair one, and then I dropped him with a quick one. I told him "get up, fight like a man you a man right?" he got up pleading- I dropped him again. "Get up; you didn't know that I knew how to fight huh?" I was messing with him. He got up and ran, I wasn't done yet so I chased him down the street while this broad was yelling my name at the top of her lungs out the window. This dude was trying to jump in cars that were waiting for the light. It was funny as shit to me. Especially when this white woman quickly reached over to slam on her passenger side seat lock before he could open the door. Then she pulled off with the quickness.

In the mean time living with her was a mission. While I was trying to pamper her, she didn't do any of those things for me. I had to talk to somebody about it so I would call my cousin and talk to him. He was having problems with his wife, but he still tried to give me advice. I was doing good as far as parole was concerned even though the dude I had was a known "asshole." One day I was chilling with my friend Toya smoking a blunt at the apartment. She was my heavyset thug stress, whenever I needed a chick to get "fucked up" I called Toya, she always came immediately with a crew of wild chicks and handled business. So while we were smoking I asked her friend to make a call for me. I had previously asked Shorty to get me the numbers and addresses to all the popular clothing line offices.

The girl got on the phone and nailed it. She was talking about the stories and shit with the lady, then she worked in that she had a friend that designed. The lady said to send him in. I kicked they're asses out and went right down there. The next day I met with the senior designer. He immediately purchased 3 designs from me. I was so happy I didn't know what to do with myself. I started thinking of how I would change things for my people now. When I told her she was surprised, but happy for me? I don't know. I gave my friend

Toya $50 for her friend for making the call for me. She said all she wanted was to smoke a blunt on me.

It couldn't have happened at a better time. I got my first check for fashion and it was mother's day. I was buying gifts for all the mothers in my life. Big balloons that had teddy bears and a bunch of other gifts inside. I bought one for her, both my grandmothers, my sister, her mother and for my Homies mother. Then I took them all out to eat at a Chinese buffet in the Bronx. I had to buy my grandmother some sneakers because she was wearing something crazy. The money was funny but it had to be done on the spot. I bought her some kicks from around the corner, they were the Sean Carters, so my family was beefing later that I bought her some "man sneakers" I didn't care, I did what I could do. It was better than doing nothing at all.

We had a good day; we went to my Homies mother church then to the restaurant. When they thought it was over, I said that we all were going to the hospital to visit Shorty mother. Shorty was surprised that I thought of that. Her mother had been in the hospital for years with a terminal cancer. She didn't get visits that often so she cried when we came. I'm sure that she cried every time people came, she did just about every time I went to visit with her. It made me feel helpless. I wanted to help her; my mother had died from the same illness.

I was always asking Shorty what can we get her, she said nothing, they feed her, but we took things over anyway. Little things. I made up my mind a long time ago to go on a crusade to get a cure for this illness because it was affecting all of our families. I prayed that she held on long enough for me to do it. I didn't express these thoughts to her, but this issue was in all my poetry that I wrote up north. It hurt me every time I seen her she was such a nice woman. Every time I went to her house when I was younger she would try to spoil me. Always telling me how cute I was and offering me things to eat. Me and her son were really tight those days.

I didn't share those thoughts with Shorty because I couldn't do anything about it and nobody really wanted to talk about it. I did. That's why I knew I would have to get rich for people to hear me about this. I was in a race against time and the rest of the world seem to be sleep walking.

Chapter 5

"Child abuse is defined as the willful infliction of harm to one's own children..."

I started to notice her mean streak with her relationship with her son. She would beat Lil Man ass every day from the day I stepped on the scene. At first I was just thinking this is what mother's do, spank they kids. But after while I noticed that she made it a routine and that disturbed me. He could do or say the smallest thing and she would beat him like he stole something. The first few days I said nothing. Then one night I was sitting in the living room and she was in his bedroom beating him, he was yelling at the top of his lungs which only seem to invigorate her more. I couldn't take it no more, I just left up north hearing all types of shit- I didn't need this. Plus he was only 6 years old; she shouldn't be beating him like this. I told her to "chill" she said "that's my son, don't tell me how to raise him" so I left it alone for the moment. But a few weeks later I noticed her trying to check her temper with him more often. One day she was "trying it" my "way" she said and was not going to beat him that night. He was provoking her though I admit.

She yelled for him to go to bed, but he stood in his door way calling for her to beat him. I went to talk to him and convince him to go to sleep while he was ahead. I told him that I talked to her and she will not beat him if he went to bed. He lay on that floor and played with the phone cord that hung loosely on his room door, ignored me and continued to call for her. She could take no more she went in and gave him a whuppen. It was like his sleeping pill. Unless he got beat he could not go to sleep. Part of it I think it was because things were changing in his world and that's how he dealt with it, by acting out. He also got a whuppen daily for acting out in school or at the after care center. She was worried to death about losing her job and when he misbehaved she had to go get him and it put her work at jeopardy. She went too far though. I picked up the weight by picking him up when he was acting so she didn't have to. It was necessary at that point. But that didn't stop the whippings.

One day I was in the living room recording my thoughts for a personal documentary I was working on. The idea was to record my day to day activities as an ex-prisoner coming home, trying to find a stable income and at the same time follow his dreams. While I was talking into the tape recorder; Shorty started beating Lil Man in the next room. It sounded so brutal that it made me sick. Don't get me wrong; I grew up in a well-disciplined household. I was a handful as a child myself and my mom was more than willing to implement what she called "an old fashion ass whuppen." But he was nothing like me, the things he did was trivial compared to me, plus he was diagnosed for ADHD. I use to tell her "You can't beat it out of him." My mother used belts and the older we got, the larger the belt got. My mom even had the nerve to make me find a belt for my own ass whuppen. I would pick the smallest belt I could find; and she would laugh and then say, "Oh, no... pass me your fathers belt, yeah - the white one."

She would have me pull down my pants and depending on the severity of my offence, sometimes pull my draws down too. Turn around and place my hands firmly on the couch - and Pow! Give me a whack. She would wait patiently as I jumped around holding my butt until she would continue. When I took too long she would threaten to "tear [my] ass up" if I didn't bend over. Sometimes I would receive 5 strikes, sometimes 10 depending on how she felt and what I did. As I grew older her weapon changed to an extension cord. That is when shit got real.

Even then; I understood it was discipline... my mother didn't beat me for any and every little thing I did and she definitely did not beat me for crying when she was whipping me; she expected me to cry. Not Shorty; if her son cried or yelled louder than she thought was necessary she would lay into him even more. My mother did not always apply the belt, sometimes she talked to me, sometimes she just let it go; but not Ms. Lady. She was not only extra with it; she was also verbally abusive to her son. My mother never said some of the things to me that she said to Lil Man like "You ain't shit" or "I wish I never had you" or "Your a retard; your an ass" or "I don't want you." That can seriously damage a child in the head if he or she is told that by their parent every time that parent got angry. I believe in the old Bible saying "If you spare the rod; you spoil the child."

I believe in ass whuppings but there's a big difference between an ass whuppin and abuse. The difference is how you execute, how forceful you execute and how often. You don't beat a child with your hands either; like you in a damn street fight; you get that handy dandy "Daddy's" belt. You don't beat them all over their body attempting to hit anything unguarded. You spank them on that ass. And most of all you definitely don't take your anger out on your child. She would tell me that "You don't have a child so you don't know." I knew that I wouldn't beat my child like that. She would say "I'm not even hitting him that hard; he's just being dramatic." I stopped the tape from recording; but I decided to save it so she could hear what I heard and understand why it was wrong, why she had to stop and why it was driving me crazy. I was going to play it back for her, but I put it off for another day and it slipped my mind.

Then I noticed that she would beat him if she had an argument with his father. That really disturbed me. I told her that was wrong when I first seen it, but she did it anyway. That's when my feelings changed for her. I said to myself if she could treat her son this way she will do it to anybody. I asked her how she would feel if it was done to her she acted like she didn't care. I thought talking to her about it would enlighten her about the damage she was causing the boy beating him every day. I told her when he got older he was going to whup her ass she put on a evil smile and said "well that's why I'm getting mine now" then went and slapped him again to shut up. I almost smacked her that day; I decided to smoke it off. That leaded to my habit of chain smoking. When the cigarettes couldn't do it I started smoking trees. I soon began to chain smoke hoping she would see that she was changing me for the worst. I didn't smoke anything when I first came home.

Now that I think about it; she really started acting crazy the second time I went to live with her. The first time she was basically on her best behavior. It seemed as if she was just looking for any reason to argue. It's funny what you can grow accustom to over time. Once upon a time I never argued with anyone, now I'm arguing on a regular basis. Being trapped in a situation like this is also very challenging. I could not just pick up and leave with parole on my back; plus I couldn't just go anywhere, my options were very limited. She took advantage of that. When a person believes that you need them more than they need you; they start holding things over your head. They treat you like a stepchild, like you owe them something. I knew it could be much worse; some women call your parole officer and try to get dudes violated.

Some people will do just about anything to get what they want or just to be evil. She never even threatened to call my P.O. but she didn't have to. She just made me feel uncomfortable living with her, knowing that any day she could put me out. Hospitality was dead and stinking. I believed that she was taking out her past failed relationships on me, I didn't do anything to her to deserve all the hate. I know that some people carry baggage so I told her "Don't dump your baggage on me." My hand didn't call for that and I wasn't built to pay for another man's debts. I could try to help her heal but I could not be her punching bag.

I could tell that she needed structure in her life. While she did have a daily routine, she did not have it structured. She did not know how to be responsible, especially when it came to finances. We were leading two separate lives, the only time we were working as a unit was when we were in the bedroom. I decided it was time to organize the confusion. She was the breadwinner but she would end up spending all her money on shopping for trivial things. She was a spend-aholic and by the time she received her paycheck; by the middle of the week she would be out of cash. Only having food money and transportation; absolutely no savings. I wanted to develop a system so I convinced myself to take a leadership role. Silly of me to even think of controlling a Black girl's money. It didn't matter that it was in her best interest - in "our" best interest.

It's a universal thing, when the man is the bread winner the woman wants access and involvement. That's when it's "ours," but when the woman is the bread winner she is very hesitant about letting a man have access to "her" money. That's when it's "her's" and she does not wanting no man controlling her money. That's when all the gender roles get thrown around "Your the man; you suppose to take care of me," or "I'm not taking care of a grown ass man." All that "us" and "ours" become "me" and "mines," it's a double standard, but it always work in the woman's favor because the male ego is sensitive when it comes to being a provider. It is inter-related on how we perceive manhood; and it's a status quo. It's easy for a woman to say "He's always spending my money, he needs to get his own" and everybody would agree that he's a "bum" and that she "deserves better." In contrast; if she made little or no money, than "the man is supposed to take care of her."

I cannot say that I disagree, I do believe that the man is supposed to provide and protect his family. I believe the woman is supposed to manage the household and nurture the family. I believe that the man is the head of the household, but the woman runs it. But I am also open minded. I believe that a man makes the decisions in the house hold but should always discuss it with his woman; and if she has a better idea than his then that is what should be implemented. I believe that if a woman makes more money than a man, that's fine - it doesn't mean that one becomes less than a man if his woman makes more money. I believe that we were designed to work together, so the more money that is made the better it is for "us." The problem is - some women try to make their husbands or boyfriends feel like less than a man when she is making more money. I also do not believe in women "independence." You can be independent - when your single; but when you are in a committed relationship you are "co-dependent." A relationship is a collaboration; a team effort and there's no "I's" in "We." Other than that we're just friends with benefits. You can't try to claim me; take me off the market and be exclusive if you still want your independent status... N to the O. But that's exactly how she wanted it.

I wanted to see her trust level for me and her respect for my decisions and advice. I noticed that every time she got paid she bought something for her and her son. Usually some type of clothing, sneakers, sweater, jeans, she always came in with bags on pay day. I admit after seeing it week after week I wondered why she never thought of me, but the biggest question was why she always did that. I reasoned that she wanted to see what she was working so hard for, but it was leaving her with late and unpaid bills. She would never get out of debt that way and from what she told me she was in a "heavy debt." Even though she was working at the bank. She said that they just "Threw credit cards at her," and she was "catching them too" she would say with a smile. I told her let me deal with the income. Give me the money and let me pay the bills and take care of what we needed in the house, she thought about it for a few seconds then said "no I got it" I was offended but I said nothing. The problem was that we got an eviction notice and she was the bread winner. I had to make some calls, so did she and we both came up with the money. I had to work it off doing construction and I don't know what she had to do, or who she got her money from.

My home boy called me one day to kick it with him and go out to do something. When I went uptown to pick him up, he had me babysitting his Slide off chick while he talked to Wifey. I didn't want to be bothered but she was going with us to this party. That was good because I was packing and it's always good to have a chick with you. I thought the popo would be less likely to bother me if I was with a girl. I was always packing in NY because shit just happens and I believe in protecting myself. I didn't start any shit but in the event I needed it I didn't want it in the bedroom closet. So we were waiting on homie and his Slide kept trying to make conversation with me. We waited so long that I finally gave her some attention. She was pretty but for some reason I didn't want to talk.

He didn't give a fuck about the chick I knew that when he first told me about her. She was from Chicago and she was a stripper. He took her to a couple clubs and she made some money so he smashed it once or twice. The problem was she lived right down the street from Wifey and Wifey was extremely jealous. To the point of yelling and screaming so the whole neighborhood would know the business. She even slammed doors- loud. It was embarrassing to me and I didn't know why he went through that bullshit.

We get to the party it was my Homie sister birthday. She was a butch a real one though, she really knew how to fight like a man. When we came in she was all over the Slide, but she was being rude and nasty. Slide was scared and Homie was just ignoring it so she was under me, following me around the party. It was a house party, just a few dike chicks that were busted, Sister- and us. When we were leaving it was cold outside and there I was trying to be cute with some white Lenin on. I think that I am anemic but I never liked hospitals so I never got it looked into. I was close to Slide for body heat because we were outside waiting for a cab in the freezing cold. I think Slide had to use the bathroom and Homie told her to pee by one of the cars, he was being nasty to the girl, I didn't know why but now I know it was because he was a little jealous that the girl was under me and at the same time he didn't give a fuck about her anyway. I decided to fuck with him a little bit and I told him to take a picture of us. He did; but when he went to snap the picture I grabbed her ass. I thought she would say something or hit me or something but she didn't do anything.

He was tight. I know that now because I told her to take a pic of me and him right after, the look on his face- Priceless. I thought nothing about that neither did he and I never seen that girl since. Don't know what happened to her, and I didn't ask. A few months later Shorty found the pic in my things. I wanted to know what she was doing in my things in the first place, she ignored that. I told her exactly what happened but she didn't believe me. She was pregnant at the time and she just couldn't believe that I was out there cheating while she was pregnant. The God honest truth is I didn't. I wanted to, with different girls, not the one in that picture but I had more pressing things to worry about- like money.

That is the sole thing that ruined our relationship. From that day on she never trusted me, and she made it clear. She didn't trust me before she just didn't have a reason to display her distrust. Now it was open season. She openly investigated my every move and every day she brought up that girl.

I was actually getting Homie back for what he did with her and she stumbled into it. It was no big deal to me because I knew what happened, but to her it was something else altogether. I mean everyday for years- and I am not over exaggerating.

She had this thing she use to do all the time that I picked up on quickly. She would play songs; this one in particular when she wanted me to get out. I thought I would remember that song for the rest of my life as many times as she played it, back to back, but I cannot for the life of me remember that song now. All I remember is the beginning when the chick was talking she said something like "pack up your things take your baby and leave." I was offended but I didn't say anything, I pretended that I was stupid and didn't know it was for me.

She was supposed to meet me in the Bronx at this program I had to go to. She was meeting me there for some reason I don't remember why, but we were walking down the street it was crowded out there. It was a lot of stores; this was a main strip in the Bronx for shopping. She was walking ahead of me, I could see there was a drunk women ahead arguing with this huge Puerto Rican man. She had a patch over her eye she was short, heavy set and loud. I think the guy slapped her, I don't remember but Shorty didn't see any of this ahead of her and almost bumped into the woman. The woman turned around and started yelling at Shorty to her surprise, talking about how she was going to kick her ass. I ran up on that woman before she knew what was going on. I almost made that whole block take off running I was so angry.

When that woman seen the blood in my eyes she immediately calmed down, and I knew that was not like her, I know a lot of women just like her. She sensed danger though and that instinct put her drunk ass right in check. The lady seemed more afraid of me than that giant ass Puerto Rican man, and all I did was look in her eyes. I was mad because Shorty was pregnant and this drunk bitch was raising her hand to hit her. It took all I had not to lay that bitch out flat. I got mad at Shorty for not paying attention to what's going on around her.

Me and her son were getting closer because I was always picking him up and I was always in the house. I would not go but so far because I had bad luck with getting attached to people. Everybody I loved always seem to be taken out of my life, so I tried to not be attached to nobody so it wouldn't hurt so much when they were not around anymore. I learned that lesson when my mother died. Then on top of that I had beef with his father and that is what made it so difficult to kick it to him for some reason. That was my fault and my loss, because that was a good kid. Then me not being his physical father I kind of felt left out in a way. I pretty much let her make policy when it came to him which was a mistake on my behalf. One day when we just got in we received a visit from child welfare for a child abuse claim that his father made out. I didn't know what to expect, I was on parole, I had a rachet in the closet and I wasn't sure they were who they claimed to be. But when they showed me the paper work- I calmed down. I let them know that he was just jealous that he couldn't control the situation any more. It was his thing to put niggaz under pressure that came to see her and run them off. But to me he was a punk- period.

Now I had to get the gun out the house though, I did that very night. I end up losing a few nice things because of that bullshit. Not only that but you never know how one slight change can affect everything and it can affect other people too. Cause of that visit I took my gun to my cousin and his house got raided. It was raided for something unrelated, but he had to do the time for it. Now my drama with her has crept into my family. She never thought about that though. My family was mad at me but they didn't say anything to me about it. I didn't mean for that to happen, plus I didn't know where he had it anyway, he just took it and left. My guilt as far as he was concerned was I didn't hold him down when he did his bid. I couldn't though because I was struggling and on welfare, I didn't have lunch money let alone a dollar over.

I didn't make much money in those days so I would try to do whatever I could to add on to her quality of life. Like when we had extra material from my construction jobs, I would take it home and use it. I put some tiles in the kitchen after I came home from work as a surprise to her. I did it before she came home. She smiled and said "that's nice"

When I got a few dollars over lunch money I told her that I was going to fix the leak coming from the toilet upstairs. It was ridiculous. We had shit water dripping on us every time we had to take a shit. I patched it up and painted the whole bathroom blue. I drew a picture on the wall of a man embracing a woman inside a mansion with marble floors and pillars. I knew she loved my art so I stayed up all night so she could see it in the morning. When she seen it her look was of surprise but all she said was "oh that's nice."

There were two things that bothered me about her, whenever we had an argument or disagreement she would walk out the door no matter what time it was, snatch her son and be out. Even after midnight. She would not tell me where she was going or when she was coming back. I had to guess; and my guess is that she went to see one of her female friends. But now I have to leave room for plausible alternatives. By this time we were arguing every day for things so trivial that I can't recall what any of the arguments were about. It's possible that she took her son to her friend's house; then slid off with the guy she called her "Trick". He did have a "ride" and before I got in the picture he was having sex with her regularly.

I'm sure she felt in debt to him because he was always there for her financially. Plus he used to be her boyfriend prior to her baby's father; so he has always been in her life. This is merely suspicion; I'm not saying it is a fact because I don't know. But what I do know is we were having senseless arguments that caused her to barge out of the house frequently. To me at that time it seemed as if she was not comfortable or didn't feel alive unless there was constant chaos; I also thought it could have been a way of pushing me out of her apartment without saying it directly. Whatever the case may be she always left the house at night and would return several hours later. I didn't like that,

I never accused her of being out with another man because I didn't know for sure and did not want to appear insecure. I didn't like that, I told her that she can't run away from our issues all the time; that sometimes we would have to agree to disagree. I didn't expect her to agree with everything and I sure didn't. So when she use to leave for hours it bothered me. The second thing is she didn't have a problem going to bed angry. I did. I told her that we should never go to sleep angry with each other and I tried to apply that into our lives. She didn't add on to that ideal, but she did get pregnant quite often. That began a string of abortions because she never kept up with her birth control. To my fault or blame, I influenced her to have them because I thought we could not afford more children. I don't know how she really felt about my suggestions, but I think that it made her feel a way about me. I never demanded her to have an abortion, but I can break some shit down and facts were facts, we were struggling with the bills and responsibilities now.

One thing I noticed is she had a very dominate personality. She was a control freak and I was an Alpha Male. I broke down power structure in relationships; the patriarch being the man leader of the household or tribe and the matriarch, being the female leader of the house hold or tribe. I explained why a matriarchy could never work for me; simply because I was always a leader. I left out the fact that in order to lead you must have direction and intelligence.

She was smart in her own way; but she was nowhere near as intelligent as me. I also left out the fact that I was willing to share power with her; but initially I had to establish order. Once she accepted my leadership I would share the power; I wanted her to make decisions but first she needed to be educated properly and have direction. She was far too caught up in the role of an ordinary "hood bitch" and she treated me like an ordinary "hood nigga". Now I can act "niggarish" but I was far from ordinary and I told her on several occasions "if you want to be a bitch; be a bitch in the streets but when your at home or are in the presence of your man - act like a lady." I guess she figured that anything I had to say was frivolous.

One day we had a problem with the lock on the door. I went and got a new lock. I don't remember if I did it intentionally but I got one of those locks that you needed a key for both sides. I think the man in the store offered it and I just said okay. I'm not good in stores; I'm always in a rush to get out. I got the lock and put it on. It made it difficult for her to run out the house when she got upset. I remember one night she came home after we argued at about 1:30 in the morning she was drunk and wanted to fuck, she was being uncharacteristically aggressive in bed, it made me wonder what the fuck she was doing out there and where did she come from, but I never asked or mentioned it.

I had to see my parole officer so I took care of that early that morning. Then I went to her job to get her cell phone because I needed to be on the street and talk to a few people. I was working on a few job opportunities. I went to her job and as I approached I seen her leaving her job, she didn't see me because I was across the street. She would have seen me had she picked her head up.

As I went towards her she got on the phone. She was talking I couldn't hear what she was saying; I just knew she was talking to another man. I didn't really care though. I was just wondering how long could I walk directly behind her and she not notice. I was more upset about that because I told her that she had to pay attention to what was going on around her. She went into the McDonalds and got on the line. I went and stood beside her, she still hadn't noticed me. When she picked her head up; it looked like she seen a ghost. She quickly hung up the phone, she wanted to know how long I was there I told her I was with her since she left her job which was about two and a half blocks away. She thought I heard her conversation.

She admitted with reluctance that she was on the phone with her "trick" I did not beef with her. The reason I didn't beef is because I didn't want her to beef when I was on the phone with my female friends. I left it alone.

Physical abuse may be understood as the intentional

infliction of physical harm on another person without his or her consent in any circumstance other than self-defense. - Raymond B. Flannery Jr. PhD.

It was a day that her friend was throwing a party for her "daughter" I believed her, I didn't have a reason not to, I never lied about what I was doing or where I was going so I didn't think that she would. We were quite open with each other at first. Her friend was into throwing stripper parties, toy and sex parties, that was her "hustle" Shorty went to all her parties and I never objected, not even this night so she went out and I waited at home for her. She said that she would be in by 9. I stayed up and waited for her. I busied myself with my art. I started designing clothes; the company wanted to see what I could do with shorts. 9 o'clock came and went. When I looked at my watch it was after 10. I kept doing me, 11, 12 came and went and now I was a little worried. I didn't want to call and stress her, but I wanted to make sure she was alright. I called her, she didn't answer. I called a few times and never got a response. I was worried now, NY is crazy and she was pregnant, I was thinking that she would have called, something was wrong.

After that day on the street with that drunk chick I had become a little over protective of her. She was pregnant. I went to sleep so I would not worry. When I woke up and she still was not there, I got angry. She knew that I would worry; she had to see that I called. I was imagining her in a hospital hurt. I imagined someone tried to rob her and did something to her. I was furious when she strolled her ass in the next morning like nothing happened. She was "tired" and she "didn't want to talk" I whupped her ass. That was the first time I had put my hands on a woman. I never did it before cause I never cared enough about a woman be concerned about where and how she was. I didn't know what to do so I took off my belt and whupped her like she was a child.

I felt violated after she strolled in; went straight to the bathroom to shower; gave me one word answers or brief sentences to my questions and had me following her around the apartment. I wasn't important enough for her undivided attention. So when she got undressed and jumped into the bed - I let her have it. The first hit shocked her, she screamed, "Ah! What you doing?!" I went off as she tried to cover up with a blanket. I snatched it from her and swung my belt as if I was the Conductor of an Orchestra. I was aiming for her ass and legs, she put her hands up to stop the sting of the blows and screamed "Stop! Your hurting me!" It sounded like the very words that her son would scream every damn night, so I popped her hands too. She could no longer use her hands as a cover and she gave up. When she looked at me, what I saw in her eyes was sadness, disappointment and hurt. That is what stopped me in my tracks, that look, those feelings traveled straight to

81

my heart and mind simultaneously I didn't want to smack her for some reason. After I calmed down I felt bad; really bad.

I followed her into the bathroom and apologized with tears strolling down my face. See she had been in an "abusive relationship" with her baby father who kicked her ass all the time. That is why I didn't like him. In fact I hated all women beaters. They were the scum of the earth to me, mainly because my father was abusive to my mother and I grew up paranoid because of it. I made a conscious decision never to hit a woman no matter what, that was way before she came into the picture. I hated my father because of that very thing and there I was being him. That is what made me cry most, because I designed my life to be better than him. She was crying but she listened to me when I begged her forgiveness.

Then we had sex, and it seemed like she was so much more attracted to me that day. I was wondering while I was pushing into her, did she like that shit. We were going to have to talk about this. It was like she kept doing shit and starting shit just to get smacked. But she knew that wasn't me from the door, before I was even messing with her, everybody knew, I actually had a reputation for fighting some big dude that chose the wrong block to hit his girl. She was Spanish and he was black he smacked her while crossing the street; we were in the projects on the bench. I said "you seen that?" and ran over there, I caught him by the grocery store and commenced. He was 3 times bigger and taller than me. I was about 16 years old and looked like I was 11 or 12. But I knew how to fight really well because I hung out with older guys and all we did was fight. Fight each other and fight everybody else. Before the guy knew it my whole crew was on his ass. We stomped him out and told him to take that shit from over here.

I ran one of my friend's boyfriends from our block because he use to beat her. He never did it in front of us, but she use to tell us. She use to beg me not to approach him, I didn't understand, did she want him to stop beating her ass or not, and why did she still mess with him, he wasn't even getting money, he couldn't dress, he was a punk and let's just say that she could do better. She wanted it so I left it alone.

Now here I was beating my pregnant girl with a belt. I felt shame. That is when she could have told me anything and I would have done it. She knew it too. When she looked at me her eyes seemed to say "I got you now," that's how it felt. She had the strings now that I lost control of myself and put my hands on her. Now she knew that she could get me to explode; she knew how to get under my skin which was worse than the fact that she could have me locked up. Even more so damaged was my reputation. I did not want to be known as a "woman beater." That is the most humiliating thing for a man of my character.

I realized that I was wrong for hitting her, but I also realize that it was pent up anger over the way she carried herself, the way she spoke to me, treated me and her son. None of that mattered in the eyes of society though, and I knew it. It's like a man or woman can do all the mental and emotional damage they want so long as they don't physically strike you. She felt she could say or do anything she wanted to me so long as she didn't put her hands on me. (But that wasn't fair to me because she knew that she could not win a physical altercation with me, that's probably the only reason that she didn't haul off and smack me.) She told me on several occasions that she can say or do what she wanted so long as she didn't put her hands on me; as if it was a mental game and my response to it should be a mental retaliation. The problem is; that I don't play those type of games. When it comes to me and conflict; it's really not difficult to understand, if you violate me - I put my hands on you - period.

I made it a point not to "Start no shit" or provoke anyone because I fight different. You cannot expect a person to play by your rules when you start a fight. Just like you can't be a professional boxer and expect not to get hit. Once you open that door and step in that ring - the fight is on; I have the right to fight my type of fight, not yours. That's the way boxers get knocked out by trying to fight their opponents' type of fight; so once you start a fight in my opinion I can handle it in any way I see fit. It's really simple "If you don't disrespect me - I won't slap you." I talk and treat her with respect and I expect her to do the same - is that too difficult to ask or understand? Men get a bad break sometimes because all a woman has to say is "He hit me," and the world turns against him. It does not matter what indignities that he tolerated, it doesn't matter how long he put up with blatant disrespect or how many times he asked her to stop hurting him.

It does not even have to be true; if a woman accuses a man of striking her his reputation is ruined for life and according to the law; once she makes a complaint you will be arrested and prosecuted. After the OJ Simpson case it became a national movement to arrest detain and prosecute any defendant accused of domestic violence. God help you if you lose your temper and strike a woman; whatever she did is irrelevant - your the problem and - she's the victim.

On that first day - everything changed. That is when I decided to stay. I had been previously planning to move out on the low. She was just too disrespectful to me. I had to make it up to her and I began to pamper her more than before.

Chapter 7

We had my first child. I was late getting to the hospital because I was at my friends Bills house smoking like an Indian chief. I was knocked out on the couch when I realized what time it was. I looked at my phone and had quite a few miss calls from Shorty. Come to find out she was going in. I got to the hospital as fast as public transportation would allow. I felt really bad because I had been staying close to home the whole pregnancy and on the rare occasion that I do go out she go into labor. My baby was already introduced to the world when I arrived. I felt like the scum of the earth for missing that. For not being there with her. She looked worn out, but in a bright kind of way; I can't really describe that. I had to make it up to her. I brought as many balloons as I could afford and was extra attentive. I didn't know what I could do, but she took it easy on me that day. The day when she had every right to be angry and upset, she did not express it. She let me off the hook.

The beat goes on. Trouble seems to follow me. I like to go to 42nd street just to walk around; we did it all the time for hours at a time. I never got bored with looking at all those bright lights and people from all over the world. We go to the train station, it's me her son and my baby in the carriage. I seen this dude earlier, he wore a black fur coat with some over sized blue ached washed jean shorts. His back was to me so I didn't see his face I just thought how lame it was to be wearing a fur and shorts. We walked past him and got on the 4 train I think. We were in the train for a few stops when this same dude started acting crazy. I thought we left him on the platform on 42 until he started playing his music. Then all of a sudden he started throwing batteries. I heard the loud bang and people started moving away from him. Then he grabbed the radio and slammed it on the ground several times until it smashed to pieces. When the train stopped everybody got out except for me, my family and this one white woman. I should have got out I know, but I was enjoying the show. I said nothing I just watched him. He took that as a challenge and he stepped to me and said "I will knock you the fuck out" Right. I would have fought him but I rather clap him, you don't approach a man when he with his family.

She knew I was strapped so when he came towards me she jumped in the middle and so did that white lady. They saved his life. That slight interruption showed him what I had in my hands and his bitch ass ran out the doors and to the back cart where all the people were that was running from him. I told Shorty to go upstairs and take a cab straight home. Then I went after his bitch ass. The train was in an uproar and he was yelling "you gonna kill me?" All the other passengers started to step out the train to see what was going on; I looked at him and told him he should thank those people because they saved his ass. Then I walked away. She said it was my fault.

The second fight we had was somewhat my fault. I was with Bills niece in the apartment. We were designing over the computer. Bill is an old timer that saved my life. I had a lot of respect for Bill, and I loved him. He was like my gangsta father. He was living good in the projects back in the days. His wife was a model always traveling cross seas. His peoples were Pee Wee Kirkland, he always tried to introduce me to him but it just never happened. When he went to Rikers Island he gave me the keys to his apartment, I couldn't believe he trusted me like that. He had two cats that were exotic; I use to get them hi. He had all types of fly shit in that place that I was honored to prove to him that I was responsible enough to take care of his place while he was away. We lost contact with each other when I got locked up.

I hadn't seen Bill in years. I bumped into him on the humble. My grandmother had fainted one day in the heat and she was in the hospital. They didn't know if she was going to make it. She had Alzheimer's so her health was going downhill. I went to the hospital immediately. Her sister was with her and was mentioning that none of her children were there. I called my uncle and told him to come through, he said he would, but he didn't sound too happy about the conversation. My aunt had disowned the whole family and nobody knew where she lived. My cousin said she work in the neighborhood, I went to her job. I had Shorty with me. My aunt came down to see who came to visit her. She was so beautiful. She always was beautiful, but she didn't age at all in fact it looked like she got younger. I hadn't seen her in 10 years. I hugged her tight and then we spoke for a few before I broke the news to her that "grandma was in the hospital and she may not make it." She told me she couldn't go she said that her mother "hurt" her and she would have to live with it until she died. She didn't want to see her again in life. She said that she loved to see me though and one day we had to go out. She gave me her number and said to stay in touch. She worked in a hospital like setting; a big building that had long term housing for old and sick people.

On my way out the door I saw him. He looked small, I almost didn't recognize him. He was walking with a cane and looked much older than he should have. "Bill?" I yelled before the elevator doors closed. He looked at me and went crazy. I hugged and kissed my old god father. I pretended not to notice that he was in a hospital sick. We talked and I promised to come see him again. I did, I took Shorty with me. This was a man I loved and respected so by me introducing her to him he knew that she was special to me. He told her so too, he said "you young lady must be special cause my son don't introduce nobody to me. Nobody" he smiled at her and gave her a hug and kiss "you must be family" he then opened up to her telling her our old stories together. She listened with respect, I liked that. He pulled me to the side and said "I don't know if she for you young blood, but I like her, she is respectable and she is infatuated with you" he knew more than me about life I always took his advice. That I took as his stamp of approval. I dived.

I should add that I took him a book of my designs and told him that I changed I was not on the street and I was designing clothes now, but I needed to learn how to do it on the computer. The designing company leader told me that it was a prerequisite that "hand sketches" were not done anymore. He was so proud of me he kept smiling and hugging me. He told me that his niece did that for a living. He made the call and we hooked up. It was totally innocent. She was not my type but she was hella cool, and I liked her personality. We had designed at her home once or twice. So I invited her to the apartment to do it and meet my Shorty. Plus she had a program that she was going to install in the computer for me, show me how to work adobe illustrator, which was a difficult program to figure out. She came with her little brother who was 11 or 12 years old. We were having some good conversation and designing. I was expecting Shorty any minute now. I took off my shirt because it was hot. I'm so confused now days I don't know if I was flirting, showing off or just damn hot. But I do know that I was not attracted to this girl in the slightest.

Shorty came in and there I was on the computer with my shirt off and another woman in the house on her computer. She knew about the girl and that we were going to be in the crib designing, but when she walked through that door her face turned red and she was a black girl. I smiled when I seen her and was looking forward to introducing them to each other hoping they hit it off cause I planned on having her as a friend. She was Bills niece and she knew how to design and she was motivated and conscious. She had been to college and was very smart. It was a no brainer. Shorty walked in and slammed the door behind her- loud. She walked past us and straight into her sons room, the girl looked at me probably scared to death and said "is everything alright, should I leave?" I said "no" then I heard her son's door slam even louder than the front door. It sounded like she broke the shit off.

I was so angry and embarrassed that I ran in that room in a rage. But I paused myself just to ask her as polite as I could "why?" at that point I really didn't know why because I always took my shirt off when I was in the house; especially when it was hot. See I had a "bedroom body" from lifting iron and calisthenics up north. She started cursing bitch this bitch that, but never telling me that she was mad because I didn't have my shirt on. I found that out later. I smacked her- hard. She hit me back so I smacked her again. She went off on me- I grabbed her arms and tried to calm her down.

When I left that room my friend and her brother was long gone. I was so embarrassed. I called and apologized. Shorty was in a rage "you calling to apologies that bitch and you smacked my face- you son of a bitch" She went on and on until I had to go out. She advised me to go out when things get heated and this day I was taking her advice. I just left; I got down the hall and realized that I didn't have anything. No money no toast. I went back to get my stuff but she would not open the door. I banged but she refused. I tried my key but she had put the couch against the front door so I couldn't fit in. I spoke thru the door, "just pass me my stuff and I'm gone," "no you hit me." That was the first night she kicked me out and the last time in my mind that I would give anybody the opportunity to do that to me again.

It was winter and freezing outside, I called Homie and he set me up with a key to his step father's apartment that nobody stayed in but it was fully furnished. I stayed there until morning and got back over to Shorty house before she had to leave for work, when she came out the door- I was on her. I had about sixteen hundred dollars in my safe there, I wanted that. I burst out of the side where the elevators were so quick that she yelled and ran towards her apartment. She almost got back in but I pushed in after her only to find my sister and her kids were all there. She had traveled all night because Shorty called crying. I drove around talking with my sister and felt better afterwards, but at that point I knew for sure I had to leave, I just didn't know how or when. As for Bills niece, after that we didn't speak but a hand full of times. Then I lost contact with her totally.

About a week or two later we were talking and I said "What's going on with you?...I never put my hands on a woman before." She looked at me and smiled, I got the feeling that she enjoyed these type of confrontations. She had probably grown accustom to physical assaults from her baby's father I thought. Her brother warned me that she was "A problem" and that "she provoked most of the fights" with her baby's father. I felt bad because her son witnessed the beatings from his father as well. I called him into her bedroom one day and I apologized to him for having to be present for that. He told me" it happened before", but he didn't show any emotion when he said "My dad always hit my mom." So when she smiled it disturbed me, then she said "That's only because you never been in a real relationship before. You just never had the opportunity; but inside you were always abusive." She made it sound like I was some sadistic, drunken, insecure husband that takes his anger out on his fragile, sweet, innocent and timid wife. I told her "I have been with over 100 girls in my lifetime; why am I only "abusive" with you?" She didn't answer that, she smiled and asked "How many did you live with?"

"A lot"

"Yeah right."

She didn't believe me; but it was true. I always lived with women and we never had these type of problems. Sure we had disagreements at times but it never got to the point of disrespecting one another and certainly no physical altercations. But still I began to question myself; replaying memories in my head of past relationships to see if there was early signs of potential abuse.

I tried to build with Shorty a few times I told her that the best thing I can offer her was my knowledge. Knowledge is forever and something nobody can take away from you. I had learned a lot when I was in prison. I took my knowledge into my own hands and I slept with my books. I taught her about some Black history and gave her my opinion where we had to go as individuals and as a people. I looked forward to her wanting to pick my brain for the information I obtained. She never did. Any time we talked about anything of substance or knowledge I was always the one to bring it up. I took a particular interest in her son's education though.

I knew that I was open off her when I was out of town. I was by myself and had the opportunity to do what I wanted with another woman and I didn't have the slightest interest. I went to a bar to speak to one of my dudes. He told me to meet him there and we could talk. I did. There was a lot of girls there, a lot of them knew me or knew of me. I knew several of them too. They were all over me fighting for attention even. It made me feel uncomfortable for the first time in my life. I went outside and sat in my friend's car alone and called Shorty. I told her then in a joking manner "you know I love you right?" "Why you said that?" "Because I'm being good" "whatever" I let her listen to a song that had just came out called *"Ordinary People" by John Legend she brought the album later and we listened to it a lot,* but anyway we had a good long conversation that night. I couldn't stay off the phone with her. That didn't stop her from distrusting me though.

She was going to court all the time for her son, what she told me was the boy's father was taking her to court for visitation. She said "he don't do shit for him so why should I let him see him" I didn't know the situation so I stayed out of it. If she didn't choose to divulge that information to me than she didn't want me to know. I'm at the apt alone when the phone rang. I answered. "I need you to come pick up my property" "what you talking about?" "I'm in jail" "what?" the last time I seen her she was off to work that morning "I had a fight with his other baby's mama." "Where at?" "the court, after I left the building she stepped to me, when he told her no more talking 'handle that' she came towards me and I ragged her" "that's right, that's what you suppose to do...so how you locked up? Is she locked up too?" "no, even though she started it, after the police seen her face, they charged me" "where you at?" "In the Bronx" "I'll be right there" I had been in that precinct before. I did not feel comfortable walking into a precinct at all, for any reason, let alone the fact it was considered "police contact" which was totally forbidden while on parole. I could have been violated for that alone, but without a second thought- I went. I called Toya told her the situation and she said "I'm on my way" She came in a cab 10 minutes later and we took that same cab and got out two blocks down from the jail.

I told Toya that "if he in there; when he comes out the precinct I'm gonna get at him", she said "than I'm getting at the bitch and she think Shorty fucked up her face, I'm gonna wear her ass out" so we had the plan. When we got in there I asked for Shorty property and was told to wait. That's when I seen dude and chic. Her face was fucked up too, me and Toya was laughing. Dude didn't see me until he was leaving; they were in the back signing papers. When he seen me he got scared. I whispered to him "you know what it is- I'll meet you down the block" he immediately started yelling "what?! We can do this right here!" I don't think he knew that I actually came there to pick up Shorty stuff, he probably thought that I came just for him and panicked "don't blow it up" "don't blow it up?!!? What's up right now, we can do this right here!!" he yells at the top of his lungs, now the police was looking. He runs towards the officers desk at the same time taking off his jacket like he was about to do something. The police snatch him up, arrest him then come to me "this guy says you have a gun" "come on officer, does that make sense to you?" "But do you mind if I search you?" "go ahead" he pat frisk me "if ya'll have a beef you can't come to the precinct to settle it, if you want to fight- keep that on the streets" I was shocked as hell to hear that coming from a police officer. I smiled "tell him that" "I did, that's why he is going thru and your going home cause he's an ass hole" me and Toya both looked at each other.

He gave me Shorty property and told me to get on. He said that if anything happened to that girl when we left there that we would be responsible for it. We went straight home. I mind you; I was still on parole which meant any police contact was a direct violation that could send me right back up north. I didn't think twice. From that day on I went with Shorty to her court dates too. I even tried to catch dude over there, I had two of my homeboys walking up and down the street waiting to spot him. He never came out.

I was in a cab one day and a song came on and I immediately thought of her; it was by Mary J Blidge called "Be Without you."

I only took her to visit my Grandmother on a handful of occasions. She always behaved well in front of other people; her other side was reserved for home, it was our "dirty little secret". On this particular day I decided to buy my Grandmother some Chinese food from the neighborhood. My Grandmother was not supposed to be eating fattening foods; but she was stuck in one room all the time so just to make her happy I got her what she wanted. Shorty came with me to the store; on our way back to Grandma's apartment I spotted an old comrade that I knew from Rikers Island. My comrade had a lot of respect for me because one day he got into a serious issue with the correction officers. In an effort to maintain order the administration called in a search. During that search I attacked the officers. We were tussling for a while before they could put the cuffs on me. Since then he had a lot of love for me and I had the same love and respect for him.

We greeted each other and started talking. When I looked at her, she was staring at him in a lustful manner. I recognized it because women do it to me all the time; it was "that look." The look that said "I'm interested" without words. That look that said if I catch you on a late night when my man ain't here - we fucking. I know it because I've done it, I have been on the other side so many times that I cannot keep count; like I said I use to be "Jodi". He picked up on the look at the same time that I did, then he looked at me to see if I seen it too. You see, it's quite easy for me to read body language, especially after being in prison for over a decade. You have to pick up on the tension because when it's about to be a war in jail it's not usually verbal; it's quiet and before you know it 12 inch swords are being swung and the whole yard is battling.

I was embarrassed because her body language was a poor reflection of my status and character. Her lustful stare represented her attraction for him and distain for me. It was evidence that my fortress was weak and could be invaded willingly, and I introduced her as my woman. His reaction was of surprise, he did not expect that I could have a weak fortress because he knew my character. I did not expect it because I thought I knew her. I did not mention it to her right away... it took about a year for me to say something about it. She had started an argument and I brought it up. She looked like she was surprised that I picked up on that and gave me a half ass apology. A few years later when she was sounding off about all of my sins, I reminded her of that day and she pretended that it never happened.

> *"Victims of abuse isolate themselves from friends, family and authority figures or any person that can help to end the physical abuse. Some keep abuse a secret, possibly out of fear of retaliation, embarrassment or care and concern for the abuser, commonly known as the Stockholm Syndrome."*

One night we got into a serious fight. I don't remember what caused it; but I do remember the pounding on the front door. I was all too familiar to that sound; there was no doubt in my mind - that was the police. They must have heard all the tussling and her yelling. My heart skipped a beat and then started pounding harder; I knew that I was going back to prison. She whispered "Is that the door?" I went in the living room and looked through the peep hole. Sure nuff, there were two police officers in blue uniform. They noticed that the peep hole moved and yelled "Hello it's the police!" I went back into the room and told her to "Answer the door; they're here for you." She told me "No, I'm not answering the door." We were basically whispering. I said "Just answer it, if they take me to jail - fuck it, but they know that somebodies in here."

"Why did you look through the peep hole?!" she asked.

"Just answer it."

"No, I don't want to talk to the police." Boom Boom Boom. I go to the door and fling it open "Hello, may I help you?" The officer looked at me in the eyes; the other trying to look into the apartment. "We got a call that there was a disturbance coming from this apartment, is everything alright?"

"Yes, everything is fine."

"Is there someone else in the apartment?"

"Yes, my girl."

"Would she mind coming to the door?" I called for her "Shorty, the police want you at the door." She said "No. I don't want to." They heard her. To my surprise they said "As long as everything is alright, have a good night." They left. I guessed that they did not get a call; they were patrolling the building and heard us fighting and decided to inner vein.

Shorty was angry, she thought her neighbor called them and said "That bitch needs to mind her own business. I didn't call no one when her man was busting her ass every night. They need to stay out of my business!" Don't get me wrong, I did not want to go to jail, but that response was insane to me. And I loved her for it. She told me, "I will never put you in jail...I know how much you hate that place."

I have to be honest, that night I felt like a coward. I was not afraid of the police, I gave several officers swollen eyes and busted lips. I was afraid of being disgraced for going to prison on a "Domestic Violence" case. That was almost as bad as being a rat or a rapist - almost. Nobody at that time respected a man that put his hands on a woman, especially in light of the fact that most men in prison was yearning to be in the company of a woman. And while I was behaving cowardly, she was keeping it gangsta. She was protecting me from the law even though I was beating her ass. I loved her for it even though it was crazy. Plus I know for a fact; whatever we were fighting over - I did not start it. She was the trouble maker in the relationship.

None of her relatives would babysit the kids. I don't know why, we were offering to pay them; not much but what we could afford, but they all refused. Her aunt, the one that always watched Lil Man for her even refused. Maybe it was because they did not like what they heard about me, or they were just tired of dealing with her. Whatever the case may have been; I was forced to ask my family. To my surprise, they were more than willing to mind my child.

Now things have really changed. I'm strapping my baby to my chest to drop her off at the babysitters. I did not like that shit one bit, what if my enemies seen me like this? I was sick. Shorty was adamant on me handling the children and that was insane to me.

I was no angel; sex was constantly on my brain but I did not react to all of my thoughts. One day she asked me did I see this girl from my old neighborhood and I was honest; somewhat honest. She knew about the girl because I use to go out with her in the past (way before she was even a thought). The girl is what I would call a Gangsta Bitch; she was hood. She sold drugs and she fucked like a man. So many dudes hit that that only a fool would "wife" her. Outside of her promiscuity she was a great girl to hang out with. She was very pretty in her youth, light complexion, long straight hair, a fat ass, really pretty face and a sexy ass walk. She was easy to talk to and have a good conversation with. She smoked weed, she drank and she liked to fuck. On top of all that she was a hustler. She didn't have a problem transporting drugs or holding guns. She was a Gangsta's dream girl, and I shaped and molded her personally.

The only reason I did not entertain having a relationship with her is because she deserted me when I went to prison and while I was in prison she was fucking like she had a white liver.

Shorty knew about her because everybody knew her, she was very popular. When Shorty asked me did I see her; I could have lied and said no, but I didn't I told her "Yeah". She asked did I have sex with her and I said no which was true. I told Shorty "She did not do my bid so I only allowed her to suck my dick." That was only a half truth. I refused to fuck her because she deserted me, but she did not give me a blow job either; she put my dick in her mouth then took it out. We were not in a place where she felt comfortable sucking me off; so we left and I hadn't seen her since. Why did I make it appear to be more than what it was - I don't know. And to my surprise it didn't come up in every argument she started. Maybe because she used that information to justify something that she did or was planning to do with another man. I don't know, but what I do know is I got use to her using information that I gave her against me; but this particular issue died out. I wish it was like that for everything; then maybe we could have had a trusting, honest and solid relationship.

One day a caravan full of dudes came after me, I was jogging to the building when I noticed them- notice me. When they did the doors flung open and they piled out. I was already jogging so it didn't take much to put a pep in my step. That's when I realized if I wanted to live long enough to take care of my baby I would have to move out of NY.

That meant a couple of things to me one was my enemies knew where I laid my head, and the dudes from that van I did not recognize so that only meant that I had enemies that knew me that I had no idea existed. That's dangerous. I was cool with it though because I was ready for the bullshit. The problem was- the kids. I was worried that one day Shorty would open that door and would never know what hit her. I had to do something. On one hand I couldn't keep my shit in the house cause of parole and her baby father with his call the cop shenanigans, on the other hand if I didn't I stood the chance of not being able to protect my family.

It was one morning I don't remember what we were arguing over, I had stopped keeping count. I do remember that we argued everyday and went to sleep angry an in different rooms a few times even after I sat her down when we were not fussing and told her that we should never go to bed angry. She didn't care too much for that regard. I called my cousin immediately. She was in one ear, he was in the other he could hear her saying things so he told me "don't listen to her; you want to come and take the basement, you know it's yours if you want it" "no bro I want to leave this place altogether" "you know you can stay with ma" "where she at?" "In Florida" "ain't it hot out there?" "Yeah but its open if you want it plus ma would love for you to go out there, you want me to call?" "Yeah"

Shorty heard my end of the conversation and she knew that I had a plan to go somewhere. My mind was focused on the move so in the mean time I tried to keep a decent relationship with Shorty. The plan was to get out of dodge as soon as possible. I had about twelve hundred dollars that Shorty gave me. Some of it was the allowance for the year that she gave me after she received her income tax returns; the other portion was from a joint account that she set up for us. She did not want me to have access to her personal account; so she set up a joint account and put a few dollars in there. Once I decided to move; I took the money out of the joint account before she could. I know she knew what I was planning and I did not want her to be able to stop me. I kept the money in a safe in her bedroom. I'm the only one with a key to that safe. I kept the money and a gun in that safe along with my Social Security card and Birth Certificate.

She was acting fairly decent. We were not arguing and things were going smooth. We had some really good sex one night and when I woke up she was already long gone for work. It was the weekend, a Saturday and on the weekends when she worked, I had to mind the kids, my family only baby sat when they knew that I had to work. I got up, checked on my daughter and her son, they were both asleep, then I looked around the room and noticed that the safe was not on the dresser draw. I panicked. I searched all over the room and when I found it a wave of absolute anger flowed over me. She had broken into the safe while I was asleep. It was all bent up on the side. When I opened it - the money was gone.

I called her cell phone and she refused to answer. I woke the kids up, got my daughter dressed and took a cab straight to her job. When I walked in with the kids - she was shocked. I got on the line for her register. When I got to her window I told her to "Give me my money." She said "That's not your money, that's my money and I put in back in my account." I told her, "I am not leaving here without that money, you think you slick, you broke into my safe while I was sleep. You are a snake, you can't be trusted." She knew that I would use that money to move and she tried to block my move.

I felt that I deserved that money for all the shit I tolerated from her - and a whole lot more. I took care of the kids while she was working, I was responsible for getting them to the baby sitters and picking them up at night; usually she came with me to pick them up though. I cleaned the apartment from top to bottom and I catered to her. I received food stamps because she "Made too much" at her job according to the government; which was really a bunch of BS. Anything over minimum wage is "too much" but in reality the price of living really superseded 10-12 dollars an hour.

Still she did not have to spend her money on food unless she chose to eat out. She was the "bread winner," but she didn't share her money throughout the year. Her paychecks went to her and her son and now my daughter. When I got paid; I did what I could for everybody. I couldn't do much because I didn't make much but what I did make I was willing to share. Despite the fact her example proved that I should do otherwise.

I refused to leave her window until she gave me that money. Other customers were coming and I was holding up the line. She was starting to get embarrassed, as people started to notice that there was a problem. Her co-workers were asking her "Is everything alright?" I had Lil Man watching my daughter at the front door and I was standing to the side as she dealt with a customer. Then I skipped the line and she said "Okay" with tears in her eyes as she began to count out the money and hand it to me. She did not give it all back but she gave me most of it. I was so furious that I left the kids at her job and took off in a cab. She had to take off work and take the kids to her aunt's house.

I bought my ticket and all the while telling Shorty that I was just "going on vacation" I told that to my old timer too that I worked for in Brooklyn, he looked at me with suspicious eyes, but wished me well and a safe return. In my mind- I wasn't coming back. She rode with me to the airport with Lil Man half sleep and my daughter tucked away in the baby carriage. When we got to the point where she had to turn around, she cried. I don't know what touched me but it was powerful. I looked at her in her eyes that she tried to cover to wipe the tears away and said "I'll be back" and I meant it. Everything she did and said and made me feel was erased. I got on that plane and now it was all about us. I imagined her going home with the kids struggling, so I called even though the pilot just mentioned to turn everything off. She sounded sad but she was in a rush to get off the phone. I thought then that while I was away she had nothing but space and opportunity to see another man. Just as soon as it came it went and I listened to my head phones and tried to go to sleep. It was my first time on an airplane and it was a storm, we had turbulence for the whole ride, it felt like the plane was being hit with something continuously. I was sure then that I would die like Aaliyah. That song *"missing you"* started playing in my head. When I arrived- it was beautiful. I mean it even felt beautiful. Nana picked me up at the airport and drove me to her home. It was beautiful. Palm trees everywhere. I looked through her spacey 3 bedroom home and was so happy that I would be staying there. I couldn't wait to tell Shorty. I took my phone in the back yard and whispered to her all the details. I said "I stepped into the back yard and felt like I was in China" the walls were high where people couldn't see over them and the trees- it was exotic to a Harlem boy just leaving the Bronx. I said "you gotta come out here."

We had discussed the topic previously a few times because I was always talking about leaving NY and one time I asked her to let me take my daughter she said she was not parting with "her child". I worked her into the plan one day and she told me that she "ain't leaving" her "apartment and" her "job and security without being married" the thing was she knew I did not believe in marriage. We had discussed that one night during one of our many "pillow talk" sessions. I said "it only gives the system more authority than we have in our own relationship" she pretended like she was in agreement with me.

The sun was shining bright; it was very different from where I just came from. I went to the mall to see a lot of people. I saw some of the flyest white chicks I ever seen in life, better than the chicks on T.V. With fat asses and all that. But I could not get Shorty off my mind and I was not approaching any chicks no way, so I got on the phone with Shorty and talked the night away. We even had phone sex one night. I found that I could get a job there with the quickness to take care of the family. I called her one night; it wasn't as late as I called her previously, something like 10 o'clock. When she answered she sounded tired. I tried to hold a regular conversation with her but she just kept giving me one word responses. She kept telling me she was tired- and then I heard her moan. I said "Yo you aight?" "Yeah I'm just sleepy" we always talk the night away she would just have to get over it. Then she moaned again and I heard the phone drop. When I thought she was picking it back up, the phone went dead in my ear. I called back but it just kept ringing. My mind and my common sense knew that she was fucking, but my heart wouldn't believe it- so I pretended that day- that call- never happened.

The next day she called pretending like the call never happened either, she was talking regular and I was kind of not so into the conversation. I didn't tell her when I was coming back and she was under the impression that I wasn't coming back at all, she said she "knew" that I was going to do that. She was talking out the side of her neck because I already had purchased my ticket. I arrived in NY and went right to the apartment. She was not there yet, I looked around. I noticed two things out of the ordinary, one was a condom of a brand that I did not use and a pair of old dirty sox. I didn't mention this when I seen her, I pretended that I didn't notice anything at all.

When I seen her we spoke, but it was not too long before the arguing started. I didn't come back for this. I sat her down and told her that I came to marry her and take her and the kids to a better place. She said "yes" if I ever was going to be married I thought it would be in an all-white Lenin suit with R. Kelly singing at the wedding. Some fly shit, but this would do for now until I got some money and then we would marry how I wanted to marry. I told her on that same night we were discussing marriage what I felt marriage should be. I said "I want all our elders to be there, your side of the family and mine and we go to each of them and ask for their blessing, they give us advise of how to keep our family together or whatever they think and we move on to the next one, then we jump a broom or something" I felt that it was more personal.

Our elders needed respect and to be recognized and to get the opportunity to talk to us and bless us both on our day. Even to speak against it if they chose to. I thought it would be better than some preacher we would have to pay or some court room that wanted to shuffle us out of there sooner than later. But my ideas for marriage were not accepted as real so she never entertained the thought. What she didn't understand then or now was my thoughts were all I had all that they could not take away from me. It meant a lot for me to have my thoughts respected because it made me the master of my own destiny. I did not believe in the system of justice that governed over us nor did I believe that other people should dictate to me what I should be doing. Mostly because I found that the majority of people suffered from hypocrisy. It has been my experience that other people friends and family alike don't always have your best interest at heart. I started to do with her what I only did with a hand full of people in my life time- I opened up.

I told her stories about my child hood and growing up in juvenile facilities where the staff thought "restraining" you was a few rapid blows to the face and my family keeping me inside there just to be in control of spending the money I received from my late mothers SSI checks. How they tried to keep me in there to make sure they got it all. How I ran away from the family when my mother was on her death bed, and that I never seen my mother deceased. A tear or two slipped from my eyes when I told her of my last conversation with my mom and how I hated myself for not being stronger, not staying. She told me about her pain of growing up with a mother that lost her mind over a man-her dad. How she would never allow a man to affect her like that. She never was very detailed about what her father was doing to cause her mother so much strife, all I knew is he was "abusive and on drugs." That was not uncommon to me though. I looked at her that night, we had some good sex and I was feeling her and I told her that "I have a lot of healing to do and so do you, let's spend our lives healing one another" I thought that meant something to her because what it meant to me was I knew that we had problems that have left wounds and I would do all I can to help her heal those wounds. I knew we would have to first start by talking about them that is why I was always the one to strike up most of the conversations that we did have.

I figured that if we healed each other then we could design our lives from there as happy people, not just a ticking time bomb ready to go off first sign of trouble. I wanted to because I had a lot of shit pint up inside me that I never trusted with anyone since I was a boy. I trusted her now.

Chapter 9

"Marriage does not end the cycle of physical or emotional abuse."

She was always watching a video called "Rain down on me" by Asanti. I was wondering if she was attracted to that type of life, or if it would be a self fulfilling prophesy. It disturbed me.

Her family and friends would not come to see us married is what she told me so I had my aunt and her daughter come as a witness, my aunt was skeptical too and asked me several times "are you sure you want to do this?" My aunt was always babysitting my child and she knew about all the drama. She did not think I should be in a relationship with Shorty; but she did not voice her opinions much. She advised me against it, but she respected my decision. She knew that I felt that Black men needed to be present throughout their children's lives, and I was determined to be a good father. I also believed that the United States destroyed Black Love and I wanted to be an exception to the rule, I said "yeah" I had wrote out on paper everything I wanted in marriage and I told her to do the same. Mines were detailed- which I later found out offended her deeply. Hers were vows. Mines were a long list hers was a paragraph. When I showed the justice of the peace our "marriage agreement" and asked her to sign she looked at me and said "brother you are tripping" but was I?

She made it quite clear that she "was not leaving unless we were married." I remembered exactly where we were when we had a serious discussion about getting married. We were sitting in her living room when she told me "If you marry me; if you be my husband I would submit to you." She agreed that she was difficult to get along with. I was feeling that, but I told her "I don't need you to be submissive. I need you to welcome my leadership because I will not lead you wrong. I need you to work with me, I do not want to argue or bicker. I have a lot to accomplish in life and I need you to be supportive. I need you to follow my directions, trust my judgment and contribute you own ideas." I thought that was keeping it real. I was serious, but everything she told me was just words.

When we got home she started up an argument out of nowhere. I got the feeling that she was doing it intentionally, but I didn't know why until she blurted out "than I just might as well stay here, I'm not leaving." No she didn't make me come out here; marry her and then pull this shit. We were in a heated argument and I remember her saying "fuck you I will be alright, I will get mines laying on my back" "that is only telling me that you a hoe, if you want to be a hoe- go right ahead." "That's right, I'm glad I did that. I'm glad I do what I do" when she said that the first thing that popped into my head was that night I was out of town and the phone dropped. I knew that is what she was referring to, I agitated her by saying "that's why I fucked a bitch in the projects and the pussy was good." I was lying though and really thought she didn't care at all until I went to walk pass her.

She jumped off her bed with the quickness of a cat and bit me. She had her jaw locked like she was a pit bull. I was feeling two really deep passions at that very moment. I was overjoyed that she cared enough to try and hurt me because she thought I was sleeping with someone else, two I was even angrier that she had been sleeping around when I was out of town. When I finally got her off of me I could tell that those bite marks would be in my back for life, I smacked her so hard that her eyes rolled to the back of her head. My palm was open but when it landed it was the side of my hand instead of the middle of my palm. Her eye swelled immediately. I panicked. Things got out of hand and too quick. I grabbed her "I'm sorry" she was too shocked to respond. Her eye was turning red. I could not believe that it was me that did it. I was hitting a woman. Then just like story book abuse, I was begging her forgiveness. In the back of my mind I was saying to myself "she started this though." But I felt like I was on the "Walk Of Shame" following behind her in the dark of the night while she had sun glasses on. We took a cab to the hospital, I sat in the waiting room biting my nails hoping she was okay. I took her home and pampered her. We had sex and we were on our way to Florida.

We had one last thing to do. She had to go to court for permission to leave the state with Lil Man while there was an open visitation case. I went with her; home dude didn't show instead his mother came to represent him. We got confirmation that we could in fact leave because the mother couldn't control where she decided to live. The Mother asked to speak to us afterward; we went outside to wait for her. Shorty said something to me that sent chills up my spine. "They brought me to court for this shit, that's alright because now they will never see him again in life" I looked at her "You buggin' you can't do no shit like that" "Yes I can" "did you see that lady in there? She was in tears she obviously loves the boy, you can't do shit like that you get bad karma". She looked embarrassed when I told her that but said nothing.

When the lady came out I spoke to her myself "Don't worry, we will let him stay in contact with you at all times", the lady looked me in my eyes and knew that I was speaking from the heart, she burst out with tears. She whispered "thank you" I gave her a hug, she reminded me of my family members I could not be mean to this lady, but whenever I seen her son- that's another story.

Before we left I told her, "Whatever happened in NY stays in NY. Let's not take the bullshit out there. We can start our lives fresh and new; be the people that we always wanted to be instead of the people we turned out to be." She agreed.

When we got on the train, for what would be a 48 hour ride the drama started five minutes after we took our seats. "I'm going to get me something to eat" "hold on" I said to her. She immediately threw a fit I was "telling" her when she was "hungry" I didn't bother to argue with her when all those people were around us. I told her that because I didn't know if you could be out of your seat when the man came to punch the tickets. I thought she would get the point about 10 minutes later when he came and asked us to produce our tickets- but she didn't and that was the beginning of a miserable 2 day ride on the train. She didn't want to talk- nothing. I actually wanted to go to the bathroom and bless it but she was miserable the whole ride.

Then I met this young kid that wanted to buy one of my t-shirts. He was with his family, his little sister and mother and a few cousins. I spoke with the mother and she was cool, they spent $30 with me. This upset Shorty immensely, to the point where it was the initial blow to ruin my marriage. That little girl and her brothers followed me around the train all day. I didn't mind their company to be honest because she "didn't feel like talking". When we got off the train, Nana was there to pick us up. I thought she would check her attitude but she didn't and the ride to

Nanas house was an uncomfortable silence. Me and Nana tried to make light conversation and work her into it, but she just gave tight lipped one word responses. The tension was too thick so we just sat there in silence after a while.

I figured that when she seen the house it would change her mood. It didn't. So the next day when I woke up early that morning I went out to buy some groceries for the house and I asked Shorty to make breakfast for Nana. I couldn't cook and we were staying at her home rent free, I thought it would be nice if we did things for her. I would take care of her front and back yard, do the sweeping mopping and Lil Man would do the garbage. She said "no"

She wore her attitude around like it was the latest style. I was embarrassed. She was antisocial and when she did talk it was clear as day that she was being fake. She kept telling me she wanted her "privacy" that even though Nana was "so welcoming, no woman wants another woman in her space" I actually liked it like that; I wanted to stay at Nana house for a lot of reasons, the first it kept her at bay. In order to argue she had to whisper, and act fake. I was able to live with that. Two it gave me the opportunity to show other people how she really was behind closed doors. Three it gave me the opportunity to stack my paper. On top of all that I knew we wouldn't be able to afford no house like Nanas so quickly.

Her son started acting. I mean really throwing a fit. He would misbehave all the time she would beat the hell out of him. Nana couldn't believe what she agreed to. She didn't say it she didn't act no kind of way, but the next thing you know she had bought a one way ticket to New York. I took it as time for us to really have a story book romance. Look how things had changed for us over night. We were in a new city; we were living in a house that was far beyond the dirty project we had left behind, with all its human diarrhea and urine on the stair case on every other floor. We didn't have to worry about who would be trying to kick in the door. We can live like they do on the stories. Even though I don't watch the stories- we could make our own- that was my point.

I started putting her on to songs I grew up listening to like "Stair way to heaven, You are my sunshine and Family Reunion" by the O'jays. I believed those songs represented a time when there was true love between people.

We both came from broken homes, so I wanted to create a spirit and culture of family. I wanted a happy, loving and caring wife. I wanted my children to grow up in a happy home with both parents. In order to accomplish that I would show my work ethic and she would naturally fall in line right? Wrong. I had to tell her "Erase the black board; we have to start from scratch." Meaning to forget everything you thought you knew about family; we have to relearn what family truly means and our roles in the family. The great part is we can make it up as we go along. We did not have to follow someone else beliefs of what family should be. We can certainly take a few ideas from other people and apply it, but we get to design our own ethics, rules, principles, customs etc. It was supposed to be fun.

I got a job and was running home to her for my lunch break to get a quickie. I always wanted her to do that when she was working at the bank but she couldn't, so I did. And I did it every other day. I wanted her to know how attracted I was to her. This way there would be no doubt in her mind about me and my affection for her. She still couldn't stop fussing about the little girl on the train, and the picture of me holding a girls ass. She brought it up every day, I didn't understand it. She chose to "rebel" by not taking care of Nanas home while she was away. I was working two jobs now and she was home the majority of the time with the kids. Plus she was pregnant again. When I came home most days there were clothes all over the place, her panties were all over the place. What made me notice is when Nanas husband came over to check on the house, his face cringed when he spotted panties everywhere we went. He told Nana in a phone call to New York- I found that out later.

One day I threw on an old R.Kelly CD. A song called "Step in the name of love" came on. I loved that song...it was a happy song. I danced. As I danced I thought about all that I had escaped - the streets, incarceration and death. I finally got a small glimpse of freedom and peace of mind. When I first heard the song; I was watching the video on BET in a prison yard. I came a long way and for one split second I allowed myself to be happy. In the back of my mind though I was lonely. I wanted to share my victory dance with my wife, but she was angry and avoiding me. She had locked herself in the room with my daughter for some simple reason. So when the song ended; so did my brief feeling of happiness.

After all I went through with her baby's father, I come home to find that she was looking him up on Nanas computer. I asked her what she was doing that for, she came up with some lame ass answer that I can't even remember. That's how I know she was just trying to be sneaky. I told her before we left NY that she had to let her son communicate with his father I don't play with shit like that. It was not a request.

The first time I allowed Lil Man to call his grandmother we were at a mall. I gave her my phone and told her to *67 my number and call his grandmother, it caught her off guard, but she did. He spoke to her for 15-20 minutes. We were in the dining area of the mall eating Mickey Dee's. After I initiated it a few times she kept it up, I didn't keep track or nothing but don't you know years later she claimed to me that it was her idea to keep in contact with the grandmother. She had the nerve to say this to me, as if I forgot her real intentions. I did not even argue I just looked at her in disbelief, she really believed that shit or forced herself to believe it.

We went to the mall often; mostly just window shopping when we had nothing to do. One day we went into a book store and I purchased a few books, I told her that I wanted her to read "A taste of power" by Elaine Brown and "Assata" by Assata Shakur. I said the other two books were mine and I did not want her to touch them. I was initiating or setting up boundaries. Plus she was not ready for those books mentally. It was "The 48 Laws of Power" and "The Art of Seduction" by Robert Greene. Her mind was not mature enough for that type of reading material. It will only serve to corrupt her more so than she already was. She was naturally manipulative and I knew that first hand, I did not want her practicing the principles of those books against me. When I first was exposed to them I was shocked that people could be so wicked; and I studied them, not necessarily to apply it into my life, but to familiarize myself with that type of thinking so I could recognize it in others and defend myself against it if need be.

Before I would willingly give her those books to study I wanted her to read non-corrupting material, history and self-help literature. I wanted to give her a sense of purpose. I had to build up her loyalty for me and her intellect on other issues before exposing her to material like that. It's like teaching a potential terrorist how to make a bomb, you don't want to do no shit like that. First you need to establish responsibility, discipline and make damn sure they are on your side first! With her it was like we were in competition against one another; so she was not ready for that. But as sure as shit stinks; when I went to work she would sneak around and read those books. She did not even bother to read the ones I asked her to read; she was obsessed with the forbidden fruit and she displayed no respect for boundaries.

One night it was a beautiful night most of them were. I was in my own world. I wanted to watch a movie with my wife then go fuck her brains out. We had did it one night in the back yard, that shit turned me on, I was thinking about round two of that. She wanted to talk so we did. She spit out so much venom that I had to look up to see her face, it was like a smile. As if she was having a good healthy conversation. She told me in no uncertain terms and didn't stutter a word "you are cute but I had that- I had cuter than you, I had niggaz with money, way more money than you, I had all kind of dick some good, some aight, some wack. You aight but I had niggaz fuck me better than you" I stopped listening, she continued but I couldn't hear a word she was saying. When she stopped talking I was shocked into silence, nobody had ever spoke to me like that before, I was numb.

I truly didn't know where all that venom came from. I said "word. Okay" I put my head down and walked to the room and laid down, I was numb and to be honest my feelings were hurt and she knew it. She came in the room and tried to make a half as attempt to make up with me. Instead of apologizing instead she laid down beside me touched my shoulder and said "Come here" but I was not into it I said "I'm aight", she said "I'm not going to kiss your ass. Forget you then." I went to sleep.

I could talk to my Grand mother for hours. We had one of those relationships where we could talk about anything. It would start off about family and before you know it we would be talking about religion and politics. I was in the back yard soaking up the sun, pacing back and forth and talking to Grandma. I could tell that I was on the phone for a long time when I felt the heat coming from her. She was staring at me from inside the house through the glass doors. I know that she heard me saying "Grandma" from time to time, so I ignored her and continued to chat it up. When I finally got off the phone - she was angry. While doing the dishes, she slammed a glass cup in the sink and broke it. She didn't own it and I end up buying Nana a new glass cup set. She didn't come straight out with why she was pissed; I found out later that she suspected that I was using my Grandmother to make 3-way calls to other girls.

On the surface a lot of the things she did was childish, immature and petty so I ignored it, but after a while it builds up on agitation, frustration and anger. Then in addition to her childish antics, she becomes verbally abusive and deprives you of sex and any other thing that she can do to attack you, eventually you explode, and that is what happened to me. She would wear out my patients totally. I knew myself; I had a bad temper and I could be compulsive; I told her in an effort to keep the peace, I basically begged her to stop and she would not. Instead she would pretend that I was over reacting or she hadn't done anything at all and that is what drove me mad. The boiling pot would spill over because she had no pause or stop button.

She made no apologies, she was stubborn, bullheaded, stiff necked, rebellious and wicked. I didn't realize it then but she was mentally and emotionally hurting me. I didn't realize it because I thought I was tough, but in reality I was emotionally vulnerable because my guards were down. In the streets I was the bad guy but in a relationship with a woman I was not tough at all. When I could tolerate it no more I would lose control and smack her face. Then she really got to play the victim role, "You always beating me" and "I didn't do nothing." I started to imagine her at court on the witness stand crying and sniffling as she brushed tears away, "He beats me, he always beats me." I could just hear the "Ooh's and ahh's" from the spectators. I could feel the cold hard stares from the judge and jury - especially the women; and it drove me mad - insane. She lied to me; in front of my face she denied her behavior so I knew she would deny it with anybody else and make me out to be the evil villain.

She was perfect at the principles of "deniability" and I could not prove different and that is what made me feel defeated. My word against hers; and her claims that she was the hopeless battered woman. All I could do was fight back because in the end it would not make a difference one way or the other.

She started beefing everyday about me being on the phone with my friends. Mostly because they were females. And one or two of them I had a previous relationship with. It did not make sense to me because although I had a previous relationship with them; I chose her to marry and have children with. While I could have been with either of them; I decided to stay with her so an innocent phone call should not have become a big problem - the choice was made. Also, I felt obligated to maintain my friendships because of all the sacrifices that they made for me. Like my "Rider" she did everything I could ever ask while I was in prison. She smuggled me in drugs, she brought me packages every month, she sent me money, she wrote me one or two letters a day, she visited me every week. I owed her some type of loyalty. Even if that was just a phone call to listen to her problems or allow her to curse me out - I had to do it. I loved her for the sacrifices that she made for me and I wanted to return the favor. I always wanted us to remain friends and I wanted her to get to know my wife as well. I believe in Karma; and if somebody is good to you and you desert them; the Universe will make you accountable. So I would talk to my friends every now and again over the phone. I told her that I did not beef with you when you were on the phone with your friends, so leave it alone. Plus if she was cool than she would realize that my friends are her friends too. None of my friends spoke ill of her, they didn't know her to like or dislike her. I told them that she was driving me up the wall but she was "my boo". They understood. But she wanted to dictate who I spoke to and she constantly checked my phone to see who had called. That bothered me and I asked her to stop. She didn't. I told her that I didn't have anything to hide, my friends were in New York anyway so where's the beef. Plus the ladies I spoke to were too egotistical to be long distance phone anything.

She kept making problems about it that I started to stash my phone. I left it out at first because I wanted to establish trust and boundaries; she betrayed both on the spot. Soon I could not talk in her presents at all which made it hard to keep a friendship going cause I couldn't chat when I was at work all the time and me and her talk on all my breaks. At times my friends would have serious problems but I wouldn't know because the phone would ring when I'm with her and I would look but not answer it because I didn't even want the drama. Eventually my friends got tired of that shit and stopped calling completely.

I spoke with her aunt; the one that was flirting with me, over the phone one day and she started firing; rapid assaults that horrified me. She described me as a wicked devil that had control over her niece mind and when I didn't get my way I would beat her. She told me that I intentionally took Shorty away from her family so she wouldn't have anybody to help her or intervene. She told me that I took her away from her mother when I knew that she was her mother's only living child. I could not believe the picture she was painting of me, that was all bullshit and lies; and Shorty was responsible for them. She's the one that started spreading horror stories about me and everybody believed her. She did not defend me when she knew that on many occasions I argued to have her mom come stay with us. I didn't even bother to tell her aunt the true story because I did not to make her look bad; but I did defend myself and we spoke for hours. The truth is nobody could intervene anyway no matter if we were in the same city state town or house. None of them intervened when we were in New York so what was the difference really? Plus I was not even going to take her with me in the first place. I only did so after that moment of weakness once she took me to the airport.

By the time I hung up the phone her aunt confessed that she knew that her "niece is a bitch, but when she get on your nerves try to walk away. You have a daughter and how would you feel if some man put his hands on her. I'll talk to my niece because she needs to be checked." The only thing that worked in my favor was the fact that her family knew her personality so they understood what I was going through although they did not approve when things got violent. One thing was for sure she was spreading venom about me and so was her family. My good name was being ran through the mud and not only they believed that bullshit one sided story; but they spread it to anyone that would listen.

> *"Some general characteristics of parent against child violence. The child is usually under age 10, the abuse is repeated regularly, sometimes on a daily basis. The mother is identified as the abuser, she is a young adult herself approximately in her early or mid-twenties. The father who may have also been violent against the mother is approximately in his late 20's or early thirties."*

She began to send Lil Man in the room all the time. To repay her for that he began to punch holes in the wall with some loose metal object he found on the bedroom floor. He was destroying Nanas home. By the time I noticed it there were little holes all over the room walls- it looked horrible. I could not afford to have it paid for at the time- I was so embarrassed. A lot of her anger was directed at her son. Whenever she got mad he was usually the recipient of her wrath. I told her she was abusive to him, but she said that's her son and that's that. One day she called me at work and asked me to come over because something was wrong with Lil Man. I was working so I didn't want to take off she said that she had hit him and she was worried because he had a black eye. I was so angry with her that I didn't know what to do, but at the same time I felt sorry for her because she was afraid that they would take him, and she didn't mean for it to get out of hand.

I rushed home and took care of the situation. I told her to tell the bus driver that he would not be coming to school for a few days cause he fell and had to go to the hospital. She did and then I gave her the business. I told her that she could never do that again. That if she hit him they will take them both and if they took my daughter she may as well get a shovel and start digging. I told her she needed to get help for that and she agreed. But she only agreed for the moment. Nana pulled me to the side and told me that she had to stop that, but Nana had felt sorry for her too because she sounded so believable when she swore that she would never do that again.

She wanted to tell me who I can speak to and for how long. One day she started an argument about this girl I met in NY before we left. The girl owned her own studio and she was an undiscovered R&B singer, but she also worked as a paralegal. I was supposed to do some graphics for her and she was supposed to network my art for me. She sent me two pictures, she wrote some slick shit like "daddy" on the envelope. I didn't know what that was about but if she was attracted to me she never let it show; not the night I met her or on the two times we were on the phone together. I still didn't want Shorty to see that so I put it on the entertainment system. When I spoke to the girl I asked her what that was about she sounded a little embarrassed but she said nothing and we talked regular ever since. The woman was married as well might I add. When Shorty found it she acted like she had something exclusive, she even waited a few days before she brought it up. I told her what it was and left it at that. She beefed about the girl so much that I stopped all communication with her myself.

Chapter 11

She went into the silent treatment on me around this time. It would last the duration of our 6 plus year relationship I later found out. One day I went to the garbage to toss something away and I found a letter ripped to pieces. It was in her hand writing, it seemed to be enough pieces that I could put it back together so I went into the garage and pieced back together what I could. What I did read shocked and frightened me to my soul.

She spew out how much she hated me and wish that I would die. She went on to say that one day she was going to take the kids when I went to work and run away somewhere where I would never find her or my kids anywhere. From that day on I began to race home every break I got, not for sex either, now it was to make sure that she didn't take off with my kids. I brought it up in a mild conversation one day and after lying about her intentions, I told her I found the letter. From that point on not only was she silent but she would rip the letters she wrote to itty bitty shreds. She didn't want to discuss how we could make that feeling she had for me change so not only was I always uneasy, she also was harboring a deep seeded hate for me that was unhealthy. In this way none of us were in a process of healing, but constant hurting, and she did not mind living like that every day for the 19-20 some hours that we were awake. That bothered me and I told her that I could not be angry with someone for so long, we need to get along or at least try, that went in one ear and out the other.

She spoke ill of my family; telling me that my uncle had money, "but he won't do nothing for you. I'm the one that gave you money because I was tired of watching you begging people that don't give a fuck about you." She would always tell me how much she "don't like" my girl cousin because "She's ghetto." That was far from the truth; my cousin was real and one day Shorty was ear hustling while I was on the phone and my cousin told me not to "put up with her bullshit." Since then Shorty didn't like her. Anyone that didn't take her side on an issue she "didn't like". She made herself appear bigger and more important than she really was. Telling me things like "No one is going to do what I've done for you." But she did more harm than good. She allowed me to stay with her but I had to walk on egg shells because she always indirectly threatened to put me out. She gave me money, the same money that she was trying to steal back from me. That was the money I used along with my own to fix up the car that Nana's husband gave to me.

She always brought that up like she purchased the car for me. She took credit for connecting me with Phat Farm when she only got the number and address from the internet. She tried to make me believe that she set up the meeting which was a bold face lie.

Now that Nana was back Shorty wanted her own place and she kept pressuring me to start looking. I finally caved in, which in retrospect- was a bad decision. We found an apartment it seemed close to Nanas home. It had two swimming pools and a Jacuzzi on the property, plus a workout center. I thought it was a condo, I found out a year or so later that it was "the projects". The day we moved in was the day that the real her came out full fledge. I hated myself for moving.

I tried to make the best out of it. I was now working at a movie theatre and a ware house. The movie theatre job bugged the shit out of me because there were so many children working in management positions. She was giving me hell about going to work because there were "a lot of girls working there". I worked at a movie theatre that was in a mall, thinking over it now; I can see why she thought like that. It was insecurity that I didn't know she had; my chick was fly, at least in my opinion. Even the pretty ones had nothing over her because my chick was pretty and sexy, that didn't always come together. I thought she was over confident because of the way she treated other people, so I failed at reminding her how sexy she was to me. I thought I conveyed that with my attraction to her. I mean every time she turned around, I wanted some ass. I couldn't keep my hands off her. She said it herself "you want to do it again?"

That didn't stop her from accusing me of sleeping with somebody. Who? I don't know to this day, but she believed it and since she believed it was true- she punished me for it. At this point there was not even a woman out there that I was vaguely interested in. I was rushing home for all my love. A lot of women were checking for me but it made me feel uncomfortable, which in turn made them feel uncomfortable, so they kept their distance and I kept mine. At home though she didn't want to talk to me because she was sure that I was doing "something."

Her words cut like a knife and she knew all my triggers and she pressed my buttons at will. I brought her some expensive shoes one day, they were sexy, high heel shoes that she wanted for work when she got a job or for a job interview. She never got to wear those shoes. I took my anger out on those poor shoes one day when she decided to give me a tongue lashing. I did not want to hit her so I beat up the shoes that I spent my hard earned money on.

One day when she got a job interview she tried to patch those shoes up and she looked pitiful. They became flip flop shoes when they originally had straps that wrapped around her ankle. One heel was higher than the other and she tried to cover them up with her pants leg. She complained "You ruined my shoes!" I figured better her shoes than her face, but I said "Stop disrespecting me." Oh no, not Miss Lady. On another occasion we were going for a drive and she was wearing some brand new Fossil shades that I purchased for her when she started verbally assaulting me.

I cannot recall exactly what she said because I blanked out. I snatched those glasses off her face with a break neck quickness while turning out into traffic simultaneously. You will not be styling and profiling and disrespecting me at the same time; that shit don't go together. I broke those expensive ass glasses in little pieces then tossed them out my car. I was at a point where I was not asking her not to disrespect me; I was telling her. I had to take the kid gloves off because she did not understand kindness and courtesy, she only understood anger and violence.

About a year or so later I quit that job. Actually I quit on the day my son was born, I just never went back. It was too stressful working there and being an outsider because the boyz always wanted to hang out with me and offered to throw back a few beers after work, but I could never go. Imagine me telling Shorty I would be hanging out after work; I may as well get a shovel and start digging. Plus every time I came home she was upset over what I was doing there, and she was so so wrong. I started another second job that I knew would keep me out of trouble with her, it was working at an old folk's home. What could she say then? Weren't any hot girls in there. The first week was good but in the weeks that followed, her same shit came out. At this point I couldn't put my finger on why or what was bothering her so I started smoking- a lot. Not just cigarettes either. I was smoking the chronic; it kept me in a mellow mood where her temper and attitude didn't affect me as much.

The honest truth is I was addicted to her body. Maybe she hypnotized me in the beginning. I remember her saying to me "I got some good pussy; that be making niggas go crazy, you see my baby father." I don't know if I felt that way or her saying it made me feel that way, but one thing was for sure I wanted to fuck her every single day. She probably put that "roots" on me or something because I was addicted. Certain little things she did like crossing her legs before she gave me head...it just turned me on. Her head game was not that spectacular, her teeth always got in the way but I made damn sure she got plenty of practice. When I would hit it from the back she would cross her legs and I would bust her ass. She was my sex kitten; I admit that. She did not fuck like a porn star but when I was inside of her; there was no other place I would rather be.

"Pussy mouth and ass is what I call a triple threat" I got that. She did not particularly like anal but she did it to please me. I wasn't a big fan of anal either, but sometimes I wanted to get freaky. That's the purpose of marriage am I right? If you cannot enjoy your lover or spouse in any way imaginable - what's the purpose of being married? If you want to experience with sex - that is what marriage is for. If your spouse is not willing to make your fantasies come true then they open the door for infidelity.

I realized that other things open that door as well... Like when you can't communicate or enjoy your spouse company; your mind begins to wander. When she started to use sex as a control mechanism; that was an accident waiting to happen. I like filatio; and she decided that she would not give me head; she would hold out for months; but if I got another woman to do it she would be mad. You simply cannot have it both ways. I found myself telling her on several occasions "If you don't do it; then who do you expect to do it?" She would not answer. I made a code word for it since "Give me some head" sounded "Disrespectful" to her ears. I would say "Get on your womanly duties" and she would respond "We can have sex, but I'm not sucking your dick." She was really pushing her luck because I am not hard on the eyes; a lot of women throw themselves at me and if I wanted to I could have them. I was trying to exhaust myself sexually with my wife and she was making that difficult when she had an attitude.

The interesting thing is even in the Bible it says you are

obligated to fulfill your spouse sexual desires. Don't believe me? Go to first Corinthians in your Bible Chapter 7 Verse 3,4 and 5 it says: *"Let the husband render to his wife the affection due to her, and likewise also the wife to her husband. The wife does not have authority over her own body, but the husband does. And likewise the husband does not have authority over his own body, but the wife does. Do not deprive one another except with consent for a time, that you may give yourselves to fasting and prayer; and come together again so that Satan does not tempt you because of your lack of self-control."*

Therefore when she does not do her "womanly duties" she opens up a door for other women. It's a living fact. Even if she was all attentive sexually; a man can journey onto different lands. That is in his genetic make-up; men testosterone levels supersede the average woman's and that is why men think of sex 100 times more than that of an average woman. Also men has had more than one wife since the beginning of time and that too is genetic. At least I was trying to stay loyal. I had a monkey on my back; being a man first; then for being in prison for so many years. I was really behaving myself. The old me would have fucked both her friends and ran through my old neighborhood like a nigga trying to get away from the police! Every opportunity would have been another episode. She did not understand how much discipline I was exercising. By the time I was tired of all her shenanigans I was truly sick in the head and an antisocial misfit.

I'm getting ahead of myself a little bit. I wasn't completely antisocial yet but I was sick in the head and acting strange. Meaning other than myself. None of my real friends would recognize me; I was talking different and acting different - and not in a good way. Always complaining about this chick. I would never had done that before.

That's when I met big Shirley. Big Shirley was from back east and she fell in love with me day one. I liked her she was kool as fuck, she reminded me of Toya. I wish now that I never met her, but what difference would it make if it wasn't her it would have been someone else. I am not attracted to big women sexually. I'm sorry it ain't anything personal, it's just preference. Most of my real friends are big women; they seem to be more authentic and down to earth. I showed Shirley my designs and she had a look on her face like she had just stumbled onto a pot of gold. She told me about her "sister" who she said would be a perfect model for me. I said I was down because I had just received a huge package from my uncle with all the latest jeans for women and men. I had Antiques, Sevens of Mankind, PRP's True Religions-everything. Her sister would model the clothes then I will make fliers out of the pictures and post them all around.

That may have been the straw, because ever since I met them my life was boiling over in misery. The first photo shoot we took was at Nanas house. It was a good shoot. I didn't tell Shorty because I knew it would be a problem and I wanted to get the work done and suffer the consequences later. I was hoping that she would see the big picture. So instead of telling her I started doing the graphics on the pictures I took, I figured I would show her the final product and she would understand. To my disadvantage she had found the pictures in my hoodie when I went to sleep. Come to find out every time I took my clothes off, she searched my pockets for evidence. I didn't know that until I woke up being smacked with, a stack of pictures. I opened my eyes only to see her standing over me yelling like a mad woman when I seen the pictures scattered all over our bed room, I silently cursed myself for not telling her in the first place.

I broke it down to her. I told her that I didn't want to tell her at first because she always goes overboard whenever I try to get paper and there's a female involved. For example, I had a bunch of clothes men and women's wear. Whenever I seen an opportunity to network the clothes, I did it. I was always with her and the kids so I never had the space to try and bag another girl. I would make an offer when I seen an opportunity and give out my business cards but as soon as we get in the car, her lips are sealed. When we get in the house she is cold, she doesn't want to talk, and she doesn't want to be touched. The kids get cold food tonight cause she not cooking- and him, he grown. This is when I was trying to make money; this happened rather I was speaking to a male or a female. This happened when I made a sale to a woman and told her about it. I had the problem with being honest to a fault.

To prove to her that it was innocent I had the girl come up stairs and introduce herself, big mistake there, come to find out she only agreed to meet "the bitch" face to face. She got intimidated by the girl, I noticed once she laid eyes on her. She didn't know then that my loyalty to her went beyond looks, plus it just was something about her that I was more attracted to. This girl was pretty, but I was thinking more like what I could do with her, how many doors I can open with her, than having sex with her. She was white with good looks and going to school for law and business administration. I wanted her on the team. I wanted to learn what she was learning and have her be a face for the business. Negotiate deals- everything. But Shorty was going so hard over chick that I said to myself one day "fuck it" and smacked her on the ass during our second photo shoot. I really played myself because- then what? I wasn't going to take it further. She looked at me surprised "what's that about?" she asked. She was a smart girl I thought. I had been all business that must have been a throw off for her. She screamed over her shoulder "don't be touching my butt" and laughed.

I was relieved that she wasn't mad and I put myself in check. What she didn't know was in my mind I was thinking "shit I have already been punished for it I might as well see how this shit feels" and my hand responded off of impulse. She then began to get more comfortable with me as I began to feel more uncomfortable around her. I just crossed a line that I could not cross back. I tried to make it back regular but every time she was around it was tension. Shorty seems to pick up things even when she was not there. Not serious things like touching or kissing and certainly not fucking, me and chick use to just kick it when we did see each other. Usually about her man, her school, her son, my Shorty, my business, my kids.

That didn't stop the wrath of Shorty. I was accused of fucking that girl every day of my life until we parted. To this day I never fucked that girl. I even tried one day but she told me that she wanted me to break up with my wife; that only meant "no" to me. Even though I disliked my wife to the point where I couldn't stand her, I would never leave her, I knew that if she ever needed me I would be there, I couldn't even lie to the girl just to get the ass. I just didn't say shit. After that, I hadn't seen that girl for years, I was still hearing her name every day. She was the reason Shorty didn't want to cook or to clean or to suck my dick or to fuck or to be touched. She was the reason why every time we went to the movies, amusement parks, football games - anywhere, she had an attitude and spoiled the day for everybody. She was the reason why family didn't want to come over because we were always at each other's throats and nobody wants to be around that shit.

She could not stop she had an obsession. It drove me crazy, over the edge, off the wall. I smoked. Before one was out I was lighting another. I kept my mind in the cloud and stopped thinking for myself. She started making all the decisions.

After awhile our issues finally crept into the bedroom, we were not attracted to each other anymore. I mean we would do it but neither one of us got anything out of it. Don't get me wrong we had our days but they were few and far between, in our last days it went totally dead though.

At a point I told her to speak to people and make the sale. I seen some girls at the bank, they were dressed in some decent shit. I told her to talk to them see if they wanted something; we had clothes in the trunk, she said "no" I was upset but I waited until we got home and tried to explain it to her as reasonably as I could. I told her that she could not have it both ways she could not beef with me and be angry with me for trying to sell clothes, if she is not willing to do it. We needed the money and we had the stuff, was we suppose to just keep it in the closet for show and tell??? She said that she doesn't like to talk to people, news flash-neither do I; but we have to do what we have to do to survive. We were not back home in NY, we didn't have all the friends and family out there we had to make it happen and fast and on all levels. She never got that. She never saw that vision. She never supported that aim.

Now when I came home from a hard days work I would take a shower and get dressed in some decent clothing, my work clothes were raggedy, I always looked like a construction worker. She use to like the fact that I was a "cleansey dude" she told me that she didn't know any men that was so clean. I made a joke and said "yeah you use to them dirty niggaz" she laughed. Now whenever I washed up and changed clothes it was for somebody. She would be angry and have an attitude for the remainder of the day for me taking a shower and changing into decent clothes. I didn't have anything new because all my money went to bills, the kids, the house. The bad thing about that was I was always with her. I did not go out without her so who was I dressing up for? I thought it was not a big thing, but eventually it became so big that I stopped washing and putting on fresh clothes. I went outside in my work clothes. The arguments about me getting "dressed up" stopped. Even when we would go clothes shopping I would be timid about what to buy and asked her opinion. I didn't want to pick nothing out that she would think was "to nice" but she still said one day "you plan on killing the ladies huh?" I ignored her. I would get a little upset to see her put on nice clothes to go out even to the supermarket and I would look like a bum, but I never said a word about it.

There was a song that I played really loud one day I was in our bedroom teary eyed and battling depression. I was hoping that she got the message in the music it was called "We're not making love no more" by Dru Hill.

She was not a nurturing, caring, loving mother or wife. She was just as cold and calculated with her son as she was with me. While she was only verbally abusive with me, she was both verbally and physically abusive to him and I knew had she been able to whup my ass I would have been whupped out too. When things got violent between us, I was avenging her son and straightening her ass out for disrespecting me. I know that I really was hurt, but when I feel like I'm getting sad I would immediately redirect that emotion into my anger. I always thought it was a woman's nature to nurture her family...I felt cheated. She reneged on her promise of marriage from day one.

I noticed she spent more time on the phone than she did talking with me. It irked me at first but I didn't think it was a big thing. It eventually became a big thing because it never ended. It was always the phone and her friends. I never knew who she spoke to but I didn't want to ask.

I was always trying to figure out ways to make more money. I had my design thing going when I left NY so I wanted to keep working that angle. I stayed on the computer after work trying to learn the graphic programs that I had. Hours can feel like minutes when you are on the computer designing some shit and teaching yourself at that. When I got off the computer she would be angry. All I wanted to do at that point was have sex and get ready for work in the morning. She was frigid; she did not want me to touch her. "Why because I was on the computer?" no answer.

She never asked a straight up question to get a direct answer; her questions always had a hidden meaning. Set up questions so she could catch me in a lie. I realized what she was doing and it pissed me off. She did not initiate conversation much, but every time she did there was a hidden agenda or she was accusing me of something. Who wants to be in a relationship like that man or woman?

Being a man; I could not do the same because then my manhood is questioned. If I interrogated or accused her in every conversation she would tell her friends and family or future love interest "I'm so tired of him, he is too insecure, he's always accusing me of being with somebody, he's always searching my phone to see who I am talking to, he always trying to see who is messaging me on line, he's too clingy and controlling." Your good name gets dragged through the excrement. But if a woman does it it's acceptable; "Oh she's just being a woman" or "That's what women do. She just cares for you." No she's being a creep. The worst thing is when people make excuses for the bullshit, especially women; they will try to blame you for her behavior, "What did you do to make her feel that way?"

I hate people like that, always being sneaky. As soon as you put your phone down, she's waiting for you to turn your back. She swipes it when your not paying attention and lock herself in the bathroom so you can't watch her go through it. If you will sneak behind my back to investigate me; you will sneak behind my back to cheat too. That's how I felt about it. Once I realize your a creep - I will treat you like one. If you will sneak you will lie, if you lie you will cheat, if you cheat you will steal. You can't be trusted. I spent a ridiculous amount of time trying to educate her, reason with her and break her out of such habits - to no avail.

Every day it was the same routine, I would try to change the feeling but I guess I wasn't doing the right shit at the right time. My mind was fully focused on learning all I could about these programs and producing. It got worse when my cousin told me about MySpace. I told her about it one day before I started my profile, she copped an attitude "what you need a MySpace page for they only use that to get ass" I said she don't know what she talking about it has "puff daddy and all them on there, it's a networking site," like cuzzo told me. Despite her objections I started an account anyway and I put my designs up there. I made a video from a program that I was working on and put it on MySpace. I got a lot of friends, mostly because of my pictures, but that was good too as far as I was concerned. The more people that came- the more others will want to come, that's what I figured. She hated it. I was all business on MySpace all the time but she had her thoughts and so I had to feel pain. She would deny me any love or affection because of MySpace, so I gave her the password so she could be an investigator.

Now she would know for sure that I was not violating our relationship in any way. She use to get on while I was at work all day. About 7 months later we were standing in front of The Dollar Tree when she slipped up and told me that she had her own MySpace profile, that she had hers before I had mine. When I reminded her all the hell she put me through over starting a MySpace page she says that she don't even get on hers no more. That she forgot her password. I was mortified. Maybe you don't understand, because she never did. She punished me for having a MySpace page she punished me for wanting a MySpace page she punished me for getting on MySpace period-everyday. What do I mean by punish, she denied me every facet of her affection, she made me feel unwanted she made me feel undesirable she did not want to be touched so our sex was wack. I was all of a sudden in a rush to get off of her. This is my wife, the only pussy I'm supposed to fuck for the rest of my life and I can't enjoy it because she wants to be mad all day and night, that's not attractive.

Every time I touched her she sucked her teeth so I got tired of that. She had the password anyway, some of the chicks use to say hot shit and she would be mad at me for that. I can't control what other people say. Plus this is a computer. These chicks were all in different states, what real harm were they to us? I had no privacy at that point, none at all. Not even to go to the bathroom. I realized that one day when I seen a sex book in one of my bags. I didn't want to fuck her cause she was acting. I went to the bathroom closed the door sat on the toilet turned a few pages, put my dick in my hand then- blam! The bathroom door comes flying open. Her face looks at me like I was digging in the garbage or something. I was so embarrassed, she said "this is what you do?" I'm waiting for her to leave but she doesn't, she continues "this is what you do, the kids are up running around and you playing with your dick. Good job" it took me months to realize that she really invaded my privacy; I spent the rest of the day being embarrassed though.

She did not know how to drive. Why you ask, she would say that I wanted to use it as a control tactic. When we first came she was so in a rush to learn how to drive that instead of asking me she tried to go around me and ask Nana to teach her. I wanted to teach my wife how to drive. That's a bonding thing I thought. She must have figured that she was too nasty to ask me to do anything so she was just trying to be slick and go around me. But God don't like ugly so she went driving a few times with Nana and once she thought she had it, she tried to take Nanas car to the store alone. I wanted to teach her in my car but she didn't want that. I don't know if she was backing out or pulling in, all I know is that she crashed Nanas car and the side was all dented and smashed in. I could not afford to pay for that so she just stood stung in the face. I think because of that she cannot drive to this day. Eventually I gave her my old car and she still didn't drive. I had to force her to drive my truck. Her conscience got the better of her confidence. She never wanted to get behind the wheel after that.

She was playing music really loud one day and cleaning when a song called "They don't know" by Jon B came on. I was hoping that she got the message but the truth is that she was the one telling her friends and family all these made up horror stories about me. She gave them the gas to pour on the fire and it made matters worse between us. Instead of giving her good advice on how to save her marriage, in my opinion they just reinforced her negativity.

I was staying away from her more because every time I was in her presents she would say something or bring up a name always something negative, even if we were having a good day like a birthday party. One day she thru a surprise birthday party for me. I was overwhelmed. To the point of being shy around my family that I saw every day. I was happy that day, but she had to say something. It was a sarcastic comment she said " I shouldn't even be doing this shit, where's Girl Girl now, tell her to throw you a party" what was the since of her doing it? She spoiled the feeling completely when she said that.

When I told her about it she act like she never said it. She denied everything. I told her one day she had to admit what she does and says; so she can acknowledge it, then once she knows she has a problem she can go about changing it. I told her I learned that in an Alternative to Violence class I had to take while in prison. I would even acknowledge my faults

155

first so she could see that I was not just trying to ask her to do something that I wouldn't do myself. But she always down played everything or didn't acknowledge it at all, pretend that things never happened at all; even when I would tell her word for word, she would act like I was imagining things. I knew that I was not imaging things but it happened so often that I forgot about most things, the weed helped me with that.

Now when I'm at work we are arguing. Every time we get on the phone, everything I ask her to do, there's a problem. She would complain that she didn't have anything to do all the time. She asked to be a "stay at home mom" what did she expect? I understood though and I started giving her things to do for the business. It would keep her preoccupied and we will be progressing at the same time- it made perfect sense to me. Eventually she started beefing that she had "too much to do". I was fed up with the bullshit. I just didn't have any other girl that she thought I had or I would have been with them then. Every time I went to the gas station by myself we would have a full fledge argument. If I was not in her sight- I was doing something.

I started to think more and more about how she always pretended that she was innocent after a blow up; so I began to record our arguments on my MP3 player. Now I had evidence. I was going to spring it out on her one day so she could hear her nasty mouth self. Then I thought about her being on the stand against me and realized that I may need it one day for court too, when she tried to bring charges against me. That seemed like a matter of time, not a question of "if" - but "when?" Would you believe that that damn vulture of a woman found my MP3 player, listened to the recordings and destroyed it? She slammed it on the ground and then soaked it in water. The first time she did it, I was able to salvage it. When I noticed the crack and that it was wet I asked, "What happened to my MP3 player?" She lied with a straight face, shrugged her shoulders and said "I don't know. Don't be asking me about your stuff." I shook the water out of it and sat it in some heat and to my surprise it still worked. Eventually she got hold of it again and sealed the deal.

I told her then "you make me want to see somebody else, I may as well you are punishing me for it anyway" she continued. She became very demanding like I had to do everything she said when she said it or else. I don't operate like that and I did not want her to even think that I would. You can ask me and I will do it for you, if you demand me- I'll have to get around to it. That made matters worse because in her mind I was cheating and she couldn't even tell me what to do even though she stayed. Seems like she felt like she was doing me a favor by staying with a "cheating bastard", that's how she made me feel when I was around her. The problem was- I didn't cheat so I didn't owe her shit. She was not going to be pushing me around telling me what to do. She would never respect me if I allowed that- even for love.

I stood my ground and that destroyed something inside of her. To her defense when I came home and got on that computer I could stay stuck for hours and completely forget about a store run. I was the designated driver because she didn't have a license. I had to drive everywhere and just getting home from work, I wanted to rest my feet, and she could never understand that. She really threw a fit because of it. I mean throwing dishes and everything. One day she tried to break the computer, she threw the screen on the floor and took a hammer to the pc. I had to snatch the hammer out of her hand before she destroyed it completely. That's when I knew that I was dealing with a beast.

I tried to reason with her. I worked in the heat in 115 degree weather when in the direct sun light I worked in a yard- no shade. She didn't understand that after 8 hours of that I wanted to sit down. I would come home and she would be at the door dressed and ready with the kids. Hold on. Wait a minute; let me chill for a half hour. What?

I drove home from work one afternoon; my plan was to bend her over and rush back off to work, but when I got in she started. I cannot remember what she said but whatever it was it caused an immediate fight. I smacked her to the ground and instead of going back to work after my lunch break; I took the rest of the day off. I was far too irate to concentrate on working. Instead I decided to send her to New York. I had a few dollars saved and it was time for us to separate. She would not keep my kids; I made that clear. She didn't have a job or her own place so she had nowhere to take them or provide for them; but I did. I would never allow her to raise my children on her own no way; the way she beat Lil Man; she would never do that to my kids.

I purchased her a one way ticket on Jet Blue. Beings that it was not reserved in advance; I had to pay more; but that didn't matter as long as she was gone. She began to act civilized all of a sudden. Before we went to the airport she put it in my head that she just needed a "vacation." When she said "goodbye" at the airport; she cried, so did I but she did not see me. I had already started driving away. I thought "My wife is leaving me." But I knew that I am the one that made her go. I was not going to pay for her trip back either. That was it. I bought her a cell phone and when she arrived, she called. I was having serious problems taking care of the kids and working simultaneously. I left the kids with Nana while I worked and when I got off I would go to my apartment, work on the computer, smoke my weed and sometimes just sleep.

Amiri

The kids were a lot for Nana; I knew it but she was my only resource out there. My only family and beings that I never went out to socialize; my only friend too. Once I woke up I would go get the kids; and make a store run before we called it a night. On one of my store runs I met this girl; let's call her Alice for the purpose of keeping her anonymous. As I was leaving the Gas Station there was a White girl in her car bumping a Lil Kim CD. She was gorgeous. Natural rusty brown hair, green eyes with a model figure. She called me over to her car. She was a bit saucy, I could tell that she had been drinking. She said "You fine. I wanna get to know you." I smiled. A White guy came out of the Station and jumped into the passenger side seat of her car. I thought it was her man and was about to back up. She said "Don't worry about him; that's my friend." He nodded his head and we greeted each other. She asked, "Do you have a girl?"

"I'm married, but we're separated."

"That's better for me, you have a number?" We exchanged numbers and I drove off. A few hours later she called "What you doing?"

"I'm lying down, I have to work tomorrow."

"Do you want to do something tomorrow? Go hang out?"

"Sure why not."

The next day we met up after work. This time I got to see

her whole body. I picked her up from her job at Apple Bee's. I parked my car to get into hers. She was wearing red high heel shoes with open toes. Her feet were cute, red toe nail polish on some small manicured feet. She was leaning against the driver side door when I approached her "Come here" she asked "Can I kiss you?" She reached around and grabbed the small of my back and pulled me closer to her. I could tell that she had been drinking. I pecked her lips and then kissed her neck. I did not like kissing girls that I did not know. I was grinding against her and she got turned on. I said "Let's get outta here."

"You drive."

We got in the car "Where you wanna go?" I asked. I was not going to take her to my apartment. My kids lived there, my wife had laid her head there and even though I was disgusted with her; I had principles about territory. As we drove aimlessly listening to that same Lil Kim CD; a light bulb went off in my head. I said "I never got head while I was driving." She looked at me suspiciously then said "That's what you want?"

"Yeah"

She unzipped my pants, leaned over the seat and put me in her mouth. I was in a zone. As I drove the lights changed and I stepped on the breaks prematurely. Her head bumped into the stirring wheel. She picked her head up "You sure you can drive like this?"

"Yeah."

She put her head back down. I drove to a dead end, dark block and told her "Get out the car." She did. She had on a one piece skirt that came to her upper thies. When she got out I forcefully turned her over and she put her hands up against the hood of her car. I reached around her and began to play with her clitoris. She was moaning. I pulled down her thongs, she lifted her feet so I could get them off. I put a condom on and entered her from the back. She was slim and she had a gap. Her pussy was thick. She was moaning loud "Oh! Oh! Oh!" every time I slammed my dick into her. Her leg began to shake. I told her "Get in the car" we climbed into the back seat and she threw her leg over the head rest. I went in, I fucked that White girl like a runaway slave. She could not get enough.

The next day she called and I did not answer, so she began to leave me messages. My wife heard those messages; at least one of them before I erased them. She wanted to see me again, but I was done with that. She was beautiful - yes! I liked her personality and she knew how to fuck; but she just wasn't my wife. I had the feeling that Shorty was listening to my messages while in New York because at one point it showed on my phone "3 new voicemails" then there was only one new voicemail when I decided to check them. That was one of my bad judgment calls. I would share all of my information with her in an effort to get her to trust me more, it did not ever work and whenever a female contacted me (for whatever reason) to her that meant that I was cheating. This time she was right. I was tired of being accused without actually enjoying the experience.

When my wife called; she begged me to allow her to come back. She said that she was sorry for the way she was acting, that she knew that she was wrong but she could not control herself. This time away let her know what she was missing. She wanted her husband and children back. I was being hard on her; but honestly I wanted her back too. I did not want to be fucking random girls; I got use to the family life. Flirting was enough for me. So long as I still "had it" I could live with myself. I missed her presence and I needed help with the children. But I told her that I would "Have to think about it." She kept calling and we talked like sensible human beings. She did ask me who I was talking to out there and I said nobody; and she left it at that.

We made a plan for her return flight and she told me she was going to visit her girlfriend. I could not reach her for 3 to 4 hours afterwards. I tried to call a couple times but she did not answer. I had a feeling that she went to "do her." I believe she went to see the guy that she calls her "Trick" she told me one day that he fucked her the best out of all of her lovers. When she decided to call me back she was on her way to the airport.

"Why didn't you answer my calls?" I asked.

"I put my phone down and I didn't hear it ringing... I was at Chanell's house."

I just left it alone. I felt as if she was lying but why make an issue out of it? It was not anything I could prove, plus I had "did me," while she was away so I did not bother to create a problem over it. I prepared the house for her return. I was happy that she was on her way back. She sound cured and that was all I wanted. I got my video camera out and waited for her at the airport I wanted to capture the moment of her return. When I saw people coming out of the broad glass doors I began recording, when she came out she immediately noticed me and began walking towards the car. When she sat into the passenger seat, all that nice shit went out the window. She didn't start beefing immediately, she sat silent while I asked her about her trip. She gave me one word answers and curt sentences, "It was fine."

Then as if the thought just occurred to her she said, "I can see you were busy when I was away". I looked at her and she had that possessed look on her face, "Who was you supposed to be meeting after work? I heard the messages on your phone."

"Why were you listening to my messages? You were gone, you were not even supposed to come back, so why was you listening to my messages?"

"You didn't answer the phone when I called so I checked your messages."

"Don't come back starting up shit again." It went downhill from there. She got worse than she was before she left. I knew that having sex with someone else was not the correct thing to do for a married man even if you are separated, but with her I did not feel married. I still felt bad about it and eventually told her the truth. She of course began to ride that wave and made me feel that I should never be honest. I told her "I'm ready to stop when you are." I got that from a verse of a song by Jay-Z.

Chapter 13

Even though I worked two jobs I didn't make an extravagant amount of money she would complain about what we didn't have and what she use to do for herself when she was making the money, she didn't understand it was not just her anymore and we had to be responsible with the money. I made sure all the bills were paid and whatever extras we had left over was for the store runs she made me go on every day without fail. I still bought her the very best when I did have a little bit extra. I came in the house one day as a surprise with some coach shoes and a Fossil watch with matching glasses. She had bought me a Fossil watch in NY one time so I knew she liked them.

I took her to a concert to see Jagged Edge, 112, Lyfe Jennings etc. I went to the mall and bought her an outfit as a surprise for the event. Nana watched the kids for us and we drove out. I think that we had a drink or two, but I'm not exactly certain. But there was a long line when we arrived and while we were waiting to get in she started an argument with a guy in front of us. It could have easily gotten out of hand because she has the kind of mouth that can make you lose your cool. But I looked at the guy and he seen the ignorance all over my face. You know the "shut down the club nigga" type ignorance. Yeah that. He turned his ass around, then I told her to shut up. "Can't we enjoy one night; or do you want to go home?"

We got in and was having a good time; at least I was. Then Lyfe Jennings came on and I called my aunt (the one that use to watch my child for us in New York). She loved and adored that man, one day she said to me "If I meet him, my husband will just have to understand." It was cute to me because she was a much older woman. I called so she could hear his voice live. She did not hear so well with the crowd yelling, but she was excited when she realized who it was.

I admit that I am not a master at reading minds and I don't know the "do's and don'ts" in a relationship; or better yet the woman's rule book, so I had no idea that calling my aunt while I was out with her would make the event less special. She got angry and was upset for the rest of the night. Even after we got home and put the kids to bed.

One day she forced me to go to the store. I did not want to I was designing some shit and it was late. It was my fault though because I was on the computer all night. She was mad already so the night would not be a good one. I got up and went to the store without a word. She wanted a bottle for my daughter. I am angry and just trying to get back in the apt to finish what I was doing. As I am leaving the store there's a guy walking in I see him I walk pass him I go to get in my car. There's two girls in a car one white one a light skinned black. They said "what's up?" I said what's up they said where you from I said New York they said you cute I said thank you. Now my mind is racing, how can I let this conversation work for me and get out of here. I gave them a card and told them I sale clothes. I have all the latest I get it from NY. I am in my car now the engine is running I have my hand on the gear when dude comes back out of the store.

One of the girls, I don't know which decides to introduce us. He says "I don't know this nigga from the bottom of my shoe" I think that we all looked at him the same way. I said "what?" when he looked at my eyes I guess he decided his hands would not do so he went to reach for the glove compartment. The white girl was holding it shut, when I realized what his intentions were I pulled off and drove right home. I burst in the door grabbed my shit and went to race back out- she grabbed me. She wanted to know what was going on. I didn't have time to talk I would explain when I got back. When I went to the parking lot the police was parked behind my car. I had left the door wide open and the car running. I got there just in time. As I parked my car I noticed that the same car had pulled up in my apartment complex.

I waited I thought they followed me in there, but then they all got out of the car and started walking and talking towards one of the buildings. I waited for a second then I walked towards their direction. They were in a second floor apartment with the windows wide open. I could hear them clear as day talking about me. The white girl was saying "baby you too jealous" the dude was saying the way I looked at him I was "challenging" him, and he just came home from jail. The black girl was saying that "you was wrong that man didn't do nothing to you, you just have a complex when other men are around. He was talking to me, I'm not even your girl" I went to the door to make sure I had the right one then went home and told Shorty what happened. I decided then to move.

The next time I seen Light Skin I was walking, which was rare so I know that I was very upset and had to leave the apartment to walk it off. Light Skin pulled up beside me and asked me did I need a ride. I said "no but I want to talk to you." I told her that I knew where she lived and that I heard what she said that night. She didn't believe me until I said it word for word. Her face seemed to lose all the blood in it. I told her that I appreciated what she said, but when me and dude bumped heads again we will see how thorough he is. After she dropped me off I didn't see her ever again not in the complex- nothing. I think she moved out.

I have been accused of fucking this girl. Do you know that she has not only accused me of fucking her but did all the same things she did when she thought I was doing something wrong. Do you know how sick I was behind that? There was a dude threatening to take my life from me, her, my kids and everybody else in the world and she thinking all of that was a made up story because I wanted some ass.

She finally started a job that was at a call center. It was massive to me from the outside. She started at night shifts. Just before I got off she had to be at work, Nana watched the little ones until I got off. It was crazy I had to be to pick her up at 12-1 in the morning. I went to develop some pictures and was late picking her up one day and all hell broke loose.

She was unhappy and I knew it so I was embarrassed to pick her up at her job because I could just imagine what she says about me to her coworkers. I always wanted to be in and out without being seen.

Then I met Lili she was a hot ass. I needed my taxes done and Nana gave me a flier. It was Lili. She came over to our home, met the wife, we talked, we got into a contract and boom taxes are getting done. She was working at that time, she never worked too long a period of time because she always had to "teach me a lesson" and I'm the one who had to drop her off or pick her up from work. This woman would wear me out about me trying to make a dollar selling something, but has the nerve to come in from work with a dude's number. She had the nerve to tell me that the number was for me. She tells me that the dude seen my picture at her desk and "liked your swag" she told him what

I was into and he gave her his number so he could "get up" with me. I "got up" with him too, that's how I give it up. I made him my road dog... just to show her how the game was meant to be played; if you going to get into shit of that nature. He made songs and videos for me after that, she eventually got jealous of our friendship too.

I didn't know what she was doing with dude on the sidelines at work and I did not ask nor did I stress her about it. I had a nagging feeling that something wasn't right but until it manifest itself, I kept my mouth closed. The Lili chick was hot for me. She came over while my Shorty was at work and tried to fuck. Being the opportunist that I am instead of putting her ass out, I played with the situation. I told her to dance for me. She did. I told her to give me a show, she stripped for me and she had a fat ass. I mean one of those semi sloppy fat asses, but it bounced quite well. She kept trying to touch me and I told her to chill. I didn't want to touch her or her touch me, so I told her to lie on the floor and touch herself, she did. I started to touch myself too and watch her but she got agitated, she wanted dick. She was pushy and I felt wrong so I got up and said "we gotta go before I do something I'm gonna regret."

Back at the ranch while I was at work and Nana was minding Lil Man- he started acting up outside and Nana tells him that he had to come inside the house. He throws himself to the ground and starts balling, she goes to pick him up he throws himself to the ground again but this time he breaks Nana's foot. She calls me at work to mind the kids because her husband came to pick her up to drive her to the hospital. She ends up with pins in her foot. I gave his ass a whuppen that day. As much as I hated to I couldn't spare him for that, he could have avoided her serious injury had he listened. I explained that to him after the whuppen. Shorty lost the job because Nana was the only one we had to baby sit him but let her tell the story and I made her quit. She totally forgot about Nana, that's only because she didn't have to pay the hospital bills.

Fool as I was my conscious got the better of me and one night I sat her down and confessed all my sins. I wanted to be open and get it behind us and start from scratch, it wasn't as bad as she thought, but I wasn't squeaky clean either. I said when we confess to one another we should not use it against each other in another argument because that will make us not want to be honest later. I said this for her benefit because I was going to be honest regardless. I didn't have any more space in my head to create a lie. Instead I became a master of omission. She forced me to do that with her jealousy. We agreed not to do it, but you know that was a lie. From that day on Lili was a permanent fixture in our relationship. She didn't understand that she too had a lot to do with my decision to entertain myself with Lili. It was like I said before; I am not Jesus Christ being nailed to the cross.

If I am to be punished for a crime I may as well have enjoyed it. Like say for example a dude is walking by and the police raid. He is snatched and there's a bag with money and drugs sitting in the area. They charge him with it. He knows it's not his so when he has to do the time for it hurts him.

For him to do all that time he may as well have sold the dope and got paid. I was not being paid so I took some back pay. It was a bad decision, I knew then as I know now, but I did it and I asked for forgiveness, she never forgave me and that is why things got worst instead of better.

There was a really old song that I played in my ride for her while we were on one of her mandatory store run missions. It was called "if you don't know me by now" by Harold Melvin and The Blue Notes.

One day I decided this was her day nobody was to bother mommy. I had Lil Man help me prepare the kids a meal and I got out the foot bath I bought for her from Bed Bath and Beyond. I had cut some aloe Vera leaves earlier, so I sliced one open and the slimy liquid came out. I put her feet in the hot water and started running the massage for the feet. I got a hot bowl of water and put the bath beads in it. I took the aloe Vera and rubbed it in her face to get deep inside the pores. I went to the kitchen and got a wet white hot towel and wrapped it around her face like I seen it done in the movies. I then worked on her feet. She had the type of feet that cracked; and beings that she picked them she had gouges of skin torn out of them. They were something to work with to say the least. I worked on them feet for hours until I got them softer than a babies butt.

I video recorded us making love that day. The song "I can't sleep" by R. Kelly was playing in the background when I entered her body.

I had been running so much I neglected my family's education. I believed that had I knew some of the things I learned in prison as a child, I would not have ever made the decisions that I did. I learned of the Black Panthers read Angela Davis autobiography, Shades of Freedom, Alex Hailey Malcolm X. I had something to share I wanted to share so I sat the family down in a circle and I started reading the history books. I had Lil Man reading college book material at 7-8 years old, he was intimidated at first but I was stern, "read it" and he did and he understood what he read. I know because to get Shorty involved I told her to ask him questions about what he read. He answered correctly 90 percent of the time.

I rented videos like "Roots, and Glory" and asked him what he thought about them. I also told him that things have changed since then but we have to work hard to make something of ourselves because our history and our current circumstance demanded it. He was a smart kid; he picked up on things fast. I had him doing home work after school. He had to read a book on Paul Robeson and write a report on it. He did an excellent job. He started to take up drawing after me. I was overjoyed but I let him grow into his own lust for art, I did not want to push him and turn him off to it. He progressed faster than I did when I was a child. He brought me all kinds of art work. He started with trains and cars. He had an obsession with trains since I met him in NY.

He knew the bus and the train routes like the back of his hand. Trains that we didn't even frequent. He was my navigation system everywhere we went. His mom never really noticed until I mentioned it. She over looked him a lot, she spent too much time telling him to get out of her face to recognize that the kid had skills.

All our bills were being paid now on time- all the time. My plan was to make enough to put us in a really nice house and pay off her debt, so when she went to work she would be thinking about what she can do for "us" as oppose to what she could do for "her".

I never knew what she was doing when I was at work usually 16- 18 hours a day every day. I always worked two or three jobs at a time, now I was working at a hospital. She didn't like that, there were girls in there. Now we were going tit for tat, I didn't consciously realize that but that is what we were doing. I played private eye one day and left my mp3 player at home on record. It can record for hours; the only problem is if she moved out of range I couldn't hear what she said. I listened to her talking to her "best friend" in NY. The girl she spoke to all day every day. The girl that she admitted to me one day that she had making 3 way calls to guys so that I wouldn't see the number on the phone bill. What she didn't realize was I did not mine her talking to guys. I just would not be punished to talk to girls. I did not like this girl "her friend" but I didn't say shit or try to see who she was on the phone talking to. The girl was talking about a relationship she was having with her side chick. She went both ways and she had a man and a chick, the man didn't know about the girl but the girl knew about the man. Her side chick also had another chick on the side and she was jealous despite the fact she had a man. My wife was all into it she said that chick was tripping and then she said something interesting to me she said "you know I never told anybody about you right?" "me either" I wanted them to get into detail about what they meant by that but they never did. They started talking about something else totally.

Even though I got more out of that conversation than I would ever get from her own lips, I didn't do that no more it took too much effort too much thinking too much sneaking. I hated to be reducing myself to this but I could get nothing out of her when we talked. She never said anything; she never admitted what she was doing or acknowledged what she said.

By this time I developed a "Tick." An involuntary muscle movement, something like how people flinch when they are bracing themselves to be hit. It happened quite often throughout the day and I know it was stress related. When I thought of her or when she spoke I would flinch. When she laid down beside me, I would flinch, for any reason or no reason at all. I realized my nerves were in bad shape, but I had no idea how to stop it.

Every night we went to sleep angry at one another. I was restless. I would twist and turn through the night, then wake up 4 or 5 in the morning. I would look at her resting; she looked so angelic and peaceful. Sometimes I would whisper to her while she slept. Then I would wake her up and say "we gotta talk" she would get up with an attitude, but I thought that she would appreciate that I cared so much about getting us on the right track that I couldn't sleep through the night. I would tell her exactly what was bothering me and ask her to stop. I would tell her calmly this way we do not make an argument out of it. It was like I was begging her to be nice to me. Then after I told her what was bothering me and how we could change it, I asked her to express the things that were bothering her- she never was open about it. In fact most of the time when I woke her up it would turn out bad, we would never get to the issues because she would argue with me so I couldn't get a full sentence or thought out.

I thought it was a good idea to wake her up in the morning while the children were asleep. Plus she began to send me to work every day angry and stressing about our relationship. I began to lose focus at the job, and the guys started to notice. I started to confide in my coworker and he said that I was not "a lone soldier" everybody has trouble with their marriage. He was an older Mexican man that I looked up to and respected. He had came to America in his 30s learned English, got a job, married, raised 3 children owned 4 home's of which he lived in one of them. His advice kept me sane. I would go home after work renewed and positive, but soon as I stepped through the door, she would ruin my mood every time.

I was on section 8 at this point, she signed us both up and they gave it to me. I put her and the kids on my account. It made it a little easier. I found out that we didn't have to live in an apartment on section 8 we could get a house. She couldn't believe it. I started going in. We would go from house to house every day after I got off work looking for something nice that we could afford, and that section 8 would approve. We seen a lot of nice homes, but there was this 1 home it had 4 bedrooms and two bath rooms and a tub so big that most of the time I told people it was a Jacuzzi. When she seen it she loved it; when I asked her what she thought, she looked kind of frightened "do you think they will let us have it?" she asked. Then she said "look at your daughter she is running around like this is hers" that was it-they were going to give it to me- period. We were in a jam. I was running out of time to secure a place for my section 8 voucher to kick in, we had been looking and looking but the homes we wanted were over what section 8 would agree to.

We were dealing with a property management company that were very dismissive of us and seemed to be standoffish when they found out we were on section 8. We had been to about 10 of their properties and now I said I wanted this one. They tried to give me a hard time because I knew and they knew that they could get much more for that house than $900, so they tried to push another home on us. When I tell you that I went ape shit, I mean it. The girl that was supposed to be on our case, I made her cry so bad over the phone one day that I felt sorry for her. She didn't understand my dilemma though. If we didn't get in a place ASAP then my family would be on the street, we already let the apt complex know that we were not going to be renewing the lease.

I went in that office one day and act like I was the supervisor. The case worker brought the real supervisor in and I started telling him what to do. Nobody in that office could believe I had the nerve to go in there and make demands like I did, not even my wife. She even looked at me strange. The employees were looking at the supervisors like "what the hell!" They would not stall us out another day, I let that be clear. Sure nuff we got the house, they brought the price down and we got approved, and we moved in. It was one of the biggest accomplishments of my life. I didn't know anyone that lived in a house so nice; I think we had one of the best homes on that block. The community was a newly modeled home community. There could be no trash or weeds on our property because it was an automatic fine. I was proud, but she was not. I think that she preferred it was her instead of me and that I could not understand. Didn't she know that I was doing this for her, for the family? I pretended as if it did not bother me and I put it out of my mind, but I think unconsciously it lingered there.

I wanted everybody to see what we had accomplished. I wanted all my family members to come through and all her friends and family to come through too. The problem was that we were too far away from home. Nobody could afford to fly out there. The truth is who really wanted to though? She sat on the phone 16-18 hours a day telling all her people horror stories about me and I did the same after awhile. Nobody wants to be around a family so drama filled, so we had no visitors. We were stuck with each other. My days were the same work home get on the computer and work until I fell out at the key board. I finally decided to start my own business selling art. I put together a catalog and started networking. I was receiving some good feedback from the people that were exposed to my work.

I went on an internet networking mission. I put up profiles everywhere that it was free to operate. I was working up the momentum when she began to tear down everything. She didn't seem to want me to have my own business. One day she said something like "forget that, I will get a job and you get a job and that's all we need" that was insane to me. I planned this way before I came home, there was no way. I had a mission to raise awareness of the injustice in the penile systems and I planned to change it and hopefully get my friends out of prison, which I knew would take money, and a lot of it. Turning back on my plans was not an option; it was my life's work. The only thing I felt I could do that so many others ignored. I was necessary, my work was necessary. I seen it with my own two eyes, they were locking up miss-educated abused kids, for life. They convinced the whole nation that it was not only okay to do this but to my surprise and dismay it seemed as if the nation wanted it this way.

On several occasions I would bring up the topic and most people would say if they do an adult crime they should be treated like adults. What happened to the undeveloped mind? Isn't that why children cannot by law make certain decisions, like purchasing alcohol, and smoking cigarettes until they are respectively 18-21? On top of that we have to look at these kids lives. Lack of education means lack of information. There are things that I've done when I was 25 that I would never do at 30, that come with experience and knowledge. The system was locking undeveloped abused children away for life without them getting the opportunity to live in the first place. The nation approved, and those that did not approve could not do anything to change it. I dedicated my life to elicit that change.

I wanted her to believe in what I was doing. I thought that she would be proud of me for having a focus, having morals, principals, beliefs, goals and a cause. I went inside a uneducated career criminal, I came home an autodidactic businessman, conscious black man that planned to change the conditions of the mindset of the our people and change the mindset of the way the system viewed us. I thought that was something any woman could support, but she did not care one way or the other at least that is the way she acted. So I could not talk to her about what was most important to me.

She got another call center job and I was dropping her off at work in the morning then driving to work myself. When I finished my shift I would go pick her up. I noticed immediately that she started acting beside herself. Her attitude changed. She began to be more dismissive than normal. I had this special lotion that I use to buy for myself, it smelled really good. That was the only thing I bought for myself outside of cigarettes and weed. I bought her and the kids their own lotion and she had all her female cosmetics. When she started the job, she began to use my lotion, not only that but she would carry it in her purse with her to work. The crazy thing is when I purchased it she had an attitude, "Why you spending all that money on lotion?" is what she said to me when I put it in the cart at Walmart and told her that it was for me. When she smelled it she said "Who are you trying to impress?"

That's what popped up in my mind when I smelled her wearing it. When she got out of my truck, I noticed that she was wearing the sexy panties that I nearly had to beg her to wear in bed. To top it all off she began to wear the Coach sneakers that I purchased for her. I spent a few hundred dollars for those sneakers and it was intended for special occasions; when we went out together. But here she was wearing them to work. I don't think it would have bothered me much if she was not on my back for every little thing that I did. I could not even change clothes after work without her pitching a bitch about it and ruining my mood and my day. But she wanted to pretend that everything that she did was innocent. That is what made me extra conscious of her movements.

What could I say about it though? There's always a catch 22. If I mention her questionable movements; she can challenge my manhood, "Oh he's so insecure, he's so jealous... he's smothering me." I kept my mouth closed for the most part and she kept carrying on, dressing seductive walking extra sexy when she got out of my truck. A time or two I had to remind her that I was the one who had to drive her to work. When I noticed that her co-workers began to basically break their necks to see who I was or how I looked; I became uncomfortable with the situation and told her that she had to get Nana to chuffer her to work. She made it seem like I did not want her to work or have a job. She told people that I wanted to lock her away in the house like a slave. She totally left out what she was doing to make me uncomfortable.

She painted the picture the way she wanted and believed

her own lies. Instead of it being a case of cause and effect, she made it appear as if I did things for no reason at all. The Damsel in distress, always does the trick. Once a woman claims that she's being abused or mistreated by a man - everyone believes her without question. My problem was I could not ALWAYS be the "Bigger Person" and allow her to do or say whatever she wanted without some type of consequence.

I started smoking so much weed that I could not function without it. I kept my head in a cloud at all times. I started smoking at work. I didn't care anymore. My every thought was a way to communicate with her successfully. I had nothing else to think about aside of what I wanted to do for my business. Even the business began to become less important to me. Nothing that I came up with was successful. It seemed the more I tried, the more nasty she got. I was like spoiled milk now. I forgot about courtesy and instead of asking her to do things I just began to demand her and expect her to do it. I didn't know what the "or else" meant I never said "or else" but that's how I made it seem.

***

At this point I didn't care about my appearance, I was a smoke-aholic and I couldn't think pass go. She made all the decisions even when it appeared that I was making them. I couldn't make a decision without checking with her first, I didn't trust my own judgment anymore. She had me right where she wanted me. Depressed and tore down. I felt like a little puppy dog waiting to get yelled at and over excited for the little bit of attention that she bestowed upon me.

She didn't care about how she made me feel and she even pretended that she didn't say or do anything. For example she would curse me out like a dog then 10 minutes later come and ask me if I was hungry and if I did say yes which was rare she would toss my plate at me spilling the food. Then act as if nothing ever happened. I began to get use to her doing that. I noticed she did that with Lil Man too.

Nana and Her began to bond after Nana began to spend more time with her. Nana would drive her around to work when she had a job, to the supermarket at times and on important appointments that I could not drive her to because of my work schedule. She got into Nana's head with that "Woman Power" junk. I noticed when Nana began to make excuses for her inappropriate behavior. One day Nana told me "Shorty loves you so much." I said, "No she don't, if she did she would act like it."

"She's just venting, but she tells me all the time how much she loves and adores you." That blew my mind. She was buttering up my family! Shorty never in her life expressed those words to me. I said "She didn't tell you that."

"Yes she did. She tells me all the time how much she loves

Him."

"She never said that to me Nana."

Nana did not believe me. I was so shocked that she was telling my relatives that she loved me, I realized how diabolical and manipulative she really was. She wanted to use Nana for whatever she desired and to get on Nana's good side she filled her head with lies.

Nana began to side with her on things and feel sorry for her. It was simple to do really, girl power talk, man bashing talk to make Nana relate. Everybody has had a bad relationship and can relate or sympathize to some extent even if they haven't been through any particular issue. That can go both ways. Then she spent time with Nana and did the "girl talk" thing. I was always working so I was rarely around. She did not care for Nana, she just needed Nana to accomplish any objective that she wanted at the time. Just like the car incident, she was so nasty to me that I would refuse to drive her around. While she was in Nana's presence she got on Nana's good side. Now, when she was being an inconvenience to Nana instead of Nana realizing that I was not breaking my back to do what she wanted because of how she spoke to me and treated me; Nana would get upset and annoyed with me. Boom! She had an ally. If she spoke to me with respect than I wouldn't mind driving her around so Nana wouldn't have to be drug around for any agenda she had in her ADHD wandering mind. Nana should have told her to treat her husband in the proper manner and he will do anything you want, but that didn't happen.

Nana was such a sweet heart, she only wanted to keep the peace; she never mentioned a word to me about anything. I just picked up on things, vibes and passing statements. She knew that Nana was a sweet heart that found it nearly impossible to say "No" so she played on that. Nana never knew that I had to check her for speaking ill about Nana. She didn't say nothing too crazy but she mentioned something like "Nana don't give a fuck about you. She only cares about her own children." She was trying to get me to have animosity against Nana; but it didn't work. Sure Nana did put her children before anyone else - but what parent wouldn't? Something I needed that Nana could not do for me and she tried to use that opportunity to make me turn against Nana, "If you were her son or her daughter or her granddaughter she would have done it. You wouldn't even have to ask." She was so divisive. I checked her ass and reminded her about how much Nana did for her, for us - that none of her family members did. I should have told Nana everything Shorty had to say about her; so she could know what type of person she was dealing with - but I did not.

If I came in from work and she started beefing with me about going to the store I would intentionally make her wait for hours or I would not go at all. I only didn't go "at all" a hand full of times. I usually made sure she got to the store even if that meant we went out after midnight.

She had a legitimate beef; she was in the house all day while I was at work. But that is what she asked me for before we left NY. She said she wanted to be a stay at home mom. That was not in my plan. She had worked in a bank, I was thinking that she needed to work while I work, we stack that money, sell my designs and artwork and stack that money, start her a business too, stack that money. I wanted her to see at first how hard I was willing to work for us so she could know what she had to do for us. I just came home from prison plus I was a man so women were attractive to me, as long as I don't cheat, looking is fine. That's what men do. Some men go to strip bars; I didn't do shit like that. The most I went flirting with a female was calling them sweetheart, that is until she started flipping on me. Then I would just do shit just because. Not that I wanted any other woman cause honestly- I didn't. I just said "fuck it" sometimes.

It didn't sit right with me though because my conscious always get the best of me. I would be all conversation with the girls at work one day, they would flirt with me and I would welcome it. Then the next day I wouldn't say 1 word to them. They got tired of that shit after awhile. It was perfect for me because I already knew all of them wanted to bone me I didn't have to do it. I stuck with boning the wife even though the sex was wack now. It was always missionary style. It was no excitement for me. She made me feel like she didn't want to do it so I didn't bother with trying to please her. I would try to get off her as fast as I could. She became the next best thing from jacking off.

I turned the extra room into my office, and that is where I stayed for the whole 4-5 years that we lived in that house. I stayed to myself. I stayed working. I said "fuck it" and only came out of that room to watch a movie or go to sleep. It tore me up every day. I tried to talk to her everyday but she did not want to, she had shut down totally. I searched for ways to explain how she was making me feel and why it motivated me to start acting too.

Chapter 15

Outside of my hip-hop I would play old songs like "Love's in need of love today and Ribbon in the sky" by Stevie Wonder. I remember there was one day that we were in the car when a song came on called "blowing in the wind" by Stevie wonder, I cried because of my frustration of not being able to change the future of my people. I had read in a book written by Elaine Brown called "A taste of power" that described the struggles of my people in the 60's, that song reminded me of that book. She looked at me like I was crazy while I sung along, she never understood me.

It took a while for me to realize that she wanted full control over the kids, the house, the money, me - everything. It always was a power struggle. She despised my authority so much that every time I exercised some form of authority; she would challenge me. In an effort to teach her that we did not have to battle over power I explained to her that I am the Head of the family and she is Second in Command. I did not have an issue about her running the house. If she had told me "Take your feet off the table" or "Take out the garbage" I would have done so without argument because that is her domain. But she did not want to take orders from me as if I was not worthy or qualified for a leadership role.

She wanted to play both roles, the masculine role - making all the decisions and the feminine role when it suited her.

There in lays the problem, I'm not into reversing roles or cross dressing. Nor was I asking to be the Head of my home, some men are not worthy because they want the role without the responsibility. I was not one of those men. First I am a leader by nature, second I embraced my responsibility; I did not run from it. But instead of letting nature take it's course, she was combative and I had to control her with force. Not always physical force, but instead of a request; I had to make demands.

I asked her one day why did I always came home to an angry wife, why can't I get my back rubbed or a foot massage or a hot bath, every now and then a kind word or a smile? That never happened. It bothered me because I had done that for her when we were in NY and she was the bread winner. Even after we got our home and I was the only source of income- I pedicure her crusty feet and prepared hot baths for her. One time I even aligned rose petals in her bath on the carpet and all over the bed where we made love. She never returned that gesture, I couldn't understand why.

Her name dropping would not end. We could not have a normal day without her bringing up a name. When I tried to get pass an issue so we could build on a healthy relationship she always injected some form of negativity into the conversation - every day without fail. Along with the constant assault on my happiness she would always give me subtle threats or statements about leaving. I never felt any sense of loyalty or permanence in our marriage. Because of that I felt justified in flirting with other women and open to find a woman that would be loyal, attentive, caring, thoughtful, understanding and receptive. The problem for me was I was locked into this dreadful marriage and being pulled in two different directions. I wanted to stay with her to raise my children as a family because I loved her on one hand, but on the other I was totally depressed, angry, lonely, distraught, unhappy and wanted to get away from her.

Nobody actually witnessed her behavior because she was very careful to keep her wicked behavior away from friends and family and behind closed doors. So when I did vent with people they did not believe that she was like that. They were dismissive like Nana "Oh no She loves you" or made excuses for her behavior, "She's just acting out... She's just venting...She must be PMSing...That's how women are." I got more advice about how to make her happy than how to handle the things she did or said that hurt or disturbed me. I needed advice on how to make her recognize her inappropriate behavior and change it so we could begin to build a happy, healthy home. Unfortunately it seemed like she got a free pass to raise hell.

I began to give her control over everything. The bank accounts the bills- everything. I never double checked anything she did; she had my total trust as far as that was concerned. I was hoping she would see the big picture. I was giving her what she had denied me in NY- trust. It was my way of saying that I wouldn't ask of her something that I would not do for her myself. She never saw that picture.

One day I was talking to her attempting to make her understand the affect her constant negative and insulting behavior had on me. I began to feel like a psychologist. I would try to speak in a calm voice and reason with her. Supplying evidence of fact to support my position; but she would turn it into a shouting match in no time. She did this skillfully, she could press my buttons randomly - at will. Now we are in a heated argument. She doesn't like calm discussions that must be too boring for her, we always had to yell at the top of our lungs. It was childish, I was angry so when she called me a "Son of a Bitch!" I slapped her. She got more irate and stubborn, so instead of leaving it alone she yelled it again "Your a Son of a Bitch!" I slapped her again. She's crying now and saliva is running like a string from her tooth to her lip, "You Son of A Bitch!" I slapped her again.

I was afraid that she was going to keep saying it and I would have kept slapping her, so to try to prevent her from continuing I said, "If you keep calling my Mother a Bitch I am going to keep slapping you. You have no right to talk about my Mother."

"I wasn't talking about your Mother, I was talking about you!"

"Do you listen to the things your saying? You said your a Son of A Bitch... Your talking about my Mother, your speaking ill of the dead and every time you say it, I am going to slap you. My mother hand doesn't call for that." Sure, I was being an ass... but she never called me a "Son of A Bitch" after that day.

I took care of Lil Man more so than I did my own biological children, mainly because he was the oldest and he could talk to me and understand. My two were still babies so I spoke to him more often. He was the oldest so he was the first, the first bike went to him, the first video game system went to him, first flat screen went to him, and he grew the fastest so I constantly had to buy new shoes. I didn't want to make him feel like he was any less important than the young ones. He did get jealous like any child would his age, a lot of the times he would make the kids cry but he also was very over protective of them. He went as far as "acting like you they father" Shorty would tell them, but in truth he was picking up my slack of always being out working 16 hours a day, I was never there. Then when I did get home I went right to work on the business, he was always watching them. He was my soldier and my helper and my road dog.

Smart and mature when he was around me, when he was at school- that was another thing.

I had to leave work many days to pick him up. He was very abusive to the teachers. He even bit one teacher to the white meat; she could have had him arrested. After awhile he began to calm down. I spoke to him a lot about how to do things. Instead of beatings I said when he acts up in school or at home he was to write 100 times that he would not do that again. Then he would be free. No need to tell you Lil Man has very good hand writing now. When fewer complaints started coming home from school I knew he would be just fine.

Eventually Nana took custody of her Grandson. He was my older cousins' son; she sent him to Nana because he was headed in the wrong direction. He had been in trouble at school and was on Probation for a juvenile case. The way the kids were in New York was dangerous. They were killing each other at amazingly young ages, and she wanted to get him away from that. She asked me to look after him and I looked forward to it. I loved my family even though I was always away in some type of institution, I always wanted to be around my family, especially when I was a child being raised in the Juvenile System. If I could help to keep him away from trouble, I was more than willing to do my part. Only thing was I worked so much that I rarely had time to myself and I rarely was home.

I immediately put him to work. I would take Lil Man and Lil Cuz with me to sell T-shirt's, jeans and artwork on my rare days off. We went to barber shops; I would send them in and they would come out smiling with hands full of money. It took only a small pep talk to give them confidence. I would sit them in my truck, instruct them on what to do and send them on their mission. I wanted to give them a work ethic and it worked. They were always eager to put in work and they worked hard, even on the days when we did not make much of anything. I never told them that I would pay them, I let them assume that they were just doing a chore for me, but when I gave them a few dollars for themselves they were surprised and happy. Every time they made a sale I gave them the profit. We had good days and we had bad days, but at the end of the day they were out of harm's way and they were learning about responsibility.

Lil Cuz was a handful I admit. I grew to love him as a person as I got to know him. He was a troubled child. Like most young Black men he was raised in a single parent house hold. He had a strong Black woman for a mother, I mean monolith strong, but still she had a difficult challenge trying to raise a man. Eventually any boy would seek out a male role model. They subconsciously study the behavior and actions of men and they take on attributes that they find to be favorable; or intriguing. Beings that manhood co-relates to machismo and fearlessness, young Black males are attracted to the streets. Lil Cuz was attracted to the streets, he wanted to inject and project manhood and respect. The only problem was he needed to learn that manhood entailed more than being able to fight and having the courage to challenge anyone. I had my hands full with him, many days he was caught bullying Lil Man. I would let them play fight and exhaust themselves of all that energy that I understood boys have.

I ignored the bullying most of the time because I wanted Lil Man to be tough and stand up for himself. Plus I knew that Lil Cuz really grown attached to Lil Man and loved him like family, looked after him like his own little brother at times. But one day it got out of hand. Lil Cuz hauled off and smacked Lil Man; and I was very angry about that. I smacked Lil Cuz and asked him how did he like that? He said he didn't. I said "Don't ever smack a man, that's the greatest form of disrespect." I chastised him about being a bully, we never had that problem again. Shorty watched silently from the next room, to my surprise she did not add her 3 cents, she just observed and let me handle it. Which reminds me of something she said often about how she "Let [me] be a man." In which I always responded, "I was not asking for your permission."

What she never understood, just like most women particularly Black women did not seem to comprehend is a women cannot "let" a man be a man. That is his birth right.

When women believe that they are "allowing" you to be what nature intended for you to be they have lost touch with reality. They act as if they are doing you a favor by "allowing" you to make decisions of your family, your children. Not every woman thinks that way, but a large percentage of them do. And the women that do think that will eventually reveal their true beliefs and attempt to dominate the man. They will use anything they can to control the man: sex, children, threats, courts, family - whatever. Eventually they will end up alone or jumping from man-to-man.

It's one thing to be strong, it's another thing to be controlling. A woman that is strong is beneficial to her man or husband, a woman that is controlling is hazardous. Her belief system in time destroys her home and family. It reminds me of something I read in the Bible once, "It is better to dwell in a corner of a housetop, than in a house with a contentious woman." I often felt like there was a silent competition between us. She behaved as if our relationship was the ring or platform for the battle of the sexes.

All because of her thought pattern and belief system, she took for granted a lot of things like me treating her son like he was my own despite the fact that she would often tell me "That's my son" when I confronted her on things she did that I felt was extreme and abusive to him. Also things like working so hard to take care of all of us, paying the rent, car notes, electricity, water, phone bills, buying flat screen TV's she wanted - everything. There was no reward, positive reinforcements or encouragements, only criticism. She complained so much about what she didn't have that she did not cherish or appreciate what she did have.

I hooked up my office just the way I wanted it. When she use to get on my nerves and I didn't want her for sex I would go on the internet and check out some xxx movies. I turned the volume down so she would not hear and try to get a quick nut off. Just like the vulture that she is she picked up on it every time. She would burst in the door like she was the police; catch me with my dick in my hand. You know how embarrassing that was? She would say to me "You a nasty muther fucker, here it is you got pussy in the house and you in here playing with your self- your ridiculous" then she would slam my door as loud as she could on the way out. I got so mad that I brought a lock that I could slide on from the inside.

When she seen me putting that lock on the door- she thru a fit, she could no longer bust in the room on me. She began to keep coming back and forth so I always had to keep getting up to unlock the door. She wasn't the only reason why I locked the door, it was the kids. They always ran in my room and I smoked in there, I didn't want them inhaling the smoke. She started to bang on the door all the time like she was the police Boom Boom Boom!!! What you doing in there?! It wrecked my nerves.

I can't say that we had "good times," I will have to say we had very short lived sporadic times when we were not at each other's throats. I noticed when we were out and about she would be in a decent mood. You know how they say "the idle mind is the devils play ground?" Well it seemed like if she had any idle time she would transform into the devil's advocate or the devils maid servant; or maybe the devil herself; always serving up wickedness. Unfortunately she had nothing but idle time. We did not have multiple options of things we could do to entertain ourselves; we were on a strict - fixed budget. But still when we went out usually it was to Walmart and she would spend money that we really should have been saving. I would always rush her out of the store, it use to irritate her like you wouldn't believe but I didn't want her to have too much time in the store.

The more time she had - the more money she would spend; so I always pretended that I had something important to work on just to get her out of there. We were the "Working Poor" and I wanted to be wealthy; so my goal was to save as much as we could and invest all of our energies into business for our future. I wanted to eliminate our financial problems, put our children through school and leave them a business as an inheritance; something neither of us received from our parents.

One day while going through the refrigerator I noticed some smoked sausages. I rarely ever observed what she purchased for the house but I did recall seeing her pick up sausages on a few occasions. When I thought about it I realized that I never ate any of them and I actually like sausage and eggs with some good ol' orange juice. So I asked her, "Why don't you ever give me any sausages?" This woman had the nerve to tell me "That's for me and the kids." I was dumbfounded, but I searched my memory and realized that she didn't feed me well at all. She kept the good stuff for herself and bought special items just "for the kids," even though she ate a bit of everything. I was even out the loop when it came to the food!

She gained quite a few pounds while I lost weight. One day I looked in the mirror and was shocked by what I saw; I looked like a Crack Addict. It was the stress. I have one of those moody appetites. If I'm excited or working on something - I can't eat. If I'm about to have sex - I can't eat. If I'm upset I lose my appetite and can't eat. Beings that I was always upset - I never really ate. I wouldn't eat for weeks. I would pick at food or eat a snack but an entire meal - no.

She was in full control over what we all ate, so she knew that I was not eating; but she didn't even care. She did send me to work every morning with left over's from dinner or a microwavable meal - but that was the extent of it. She displayed no concern over the fact that I was withdrawn and not looking healthy. Her indifference when it came to me was stressful and I was too prideful to tell her about how it made me feel. I just would brush it off, put it out of my mind and keep going. I was hoping that once I was financially successful that I would be in a better space; either the issues would work itself out or I would be in a better position to leave her.

I withdrew from family life totally. I was there physically, I worked like a machine to maintain it, but mentally I was in my own world. I neglected my children and isolated myself in my home office. I did absolutely no house chores; I use to like doing house chores but I refused to help her because of her attitude and the way she treated me. Lil Man was more active with my little ones. I loved them so much - it hurt. I prayed over them every night as they slept after coming home from work. But I could not find the mental peace or energy to inner act with them the majority of the time even though I wanted to. It's hard to explain, but in some way I felt that I shouldn't get too attached to them. I focused on business as if it would resolve the problem; but really it was just my escape from reality.

The only way I could ever get her to admit to something is let it come out on its own. She never was forth coming with information. Not when asked a direct question. This one day I was talking to her and it was a decent conversation where I asked her if she ever touched herself. She said that she didn't have to she "had dick" I said come on; there have been many days that we weren't attracted to each other and your always home alone. Then she admitted that she did it a few times. That's when I realized that she had a privacy in our relationship that I did not have. She could speak to her friends on the phone and I didn't feel any way, but if I did all hell broke loose. She could touch herself and I never would know but if I touched myself she could bust in the door on me.

Now I was wondering what else she was doing that I didn't know about? Later I noticed that she liked to bend down in front of men in super markets, sneaker stores or anywhere we went together. They usually would only get to see her ass crack but that was enough when she is doing it intentionally and around me at that. But don't let me see a pretty girl passing by though. With none of the extras like looking back, she would get an attitude.

Someone once told me that retardation is defined as a person that repeatedly does the same thing but expect a different result. If her goal was to curb my interest or attraction to other women; her antics sure had the opposite effect. I honestly don't believe she even had a goal, I believe she was just rotten to the core. Like a broken record or a retarded child she would keep repeating the same thing anytime we spoke or inner acted, "You cheated. You cheated. You cheated. You cheated. You cheated." On and on, again and again and it drove me crazy. I realize now that maybe she had serious mental problems herself. She did have a retarded cousin that she was raised with, maybe it was in her DNA - mild retardation.

Whatever the case may be; living with her insanity had a deep impact and effect on me...it was contagious, because now - I'm a head case.

I told her what was going on at the hospital but it had been over a year since and I was not doing that now. One day I went to her; this was probably the 3rd time I was going to tell her the same thing. I was in a good mood I know because I figured out how we could stop the sucker shit. I said to her please stop sending me to work angry. "You do it on both jobs and you are jealous as it is, so why would you send me to the hospital with all those doctors and nurses mad with you?" I said it as a joke to make it light, but I was serious. I said that I did not ever touch anybody in there and they always are making little smart comments, even the older ones. Not so much sexual but they laughed like the rest of us at it. Oh not to leave out that all the little flirtatious remarks was not rated "R" comments and it was said in that big ass kitchen where everybody could hear. I thought it was part of the job after awhile. I kept it at a minimum and I started taking my head phones in and turning them up loud so I could not hear anything.

When she responded, she said something so nasty that when I looked at her and seen her face with this evil grit/grin, I tried my damdis to smack it off her face. It came so sudden that I didn't know what was happening. I truly blanked out. I was reaching for the phone to call Nana. "Come and get this bitch before I kill her ass in here" I didn't mean it technically but I wanted Nana to know the seriousness of the situation and rush right over. I told her that she had to leave she was to stay with Nana but she could not stay with me anymore. Then I stormed out the house and went for a long drive. I did not go to work that day. She was gone when I got back in the house. She and the kids were gone, I slept in the kid's room and I cried like a little baby. It didn't take a day to miss her, it took minutes. I don't know why though. I know that I need help with this but I don't know where to go.

I could not afford for the kids to be exposed to that. I felt like I had turned into my father. This was not how it was supposed to be. I felt like she just wanted to step all over me and then she would be happy. I felt like I was defending myself just to live, just to be me.

She conveniently forgot that there was not a long line of dudes waiting to marry her, sure they would line up to fuck her but not sign up to take responsibility to care for her and her child. So how did it make sense to push me away? Or did she think that she could do or say anything and there would be absolutely no consequence; because she's a female?

I wore my family and friends out with our relationship. I didn't have no one to vent with. I started talking to this girl from the internet. She had sent me some naked pictures so I started talking to her. Come to find out she just left her guy. She got on a bus and came to see me immediately. I went to pick her up. When I saw her in the flesh I was automatically un-attracted to her. She had a wide back and what looked like football shoulders. I said to myself "damn, what did I get myself into" I put her in the car and we drove to the house. When I gave her her own room she kind of got a hint that we were not boyfriend and girlfriend. I tried to fuck her despite the fact that I didn't have not one ounce of attraction for this girl. She seem to be having a good time, I wanted her to get off of me so I pretended to bust a nut and got up. She looked at the condom and said "there's no cum in there" and tried to grab the condom. I turned away and went to the bathroom. I missed Shorty. But Girl Girl knew how to type and work the computer and that's exactly what I needed so I started going to Nana house to break to Shorty the news of what was going on. I lied; I said the girl just wanted to rent the room for her services until she got on her feet.

I didn't count that as cheating because we were separated and I didn't like it. But that was the time that I actually violated our marriage with another woman. When I moved the family back in I tried to act regular. Now we all were living together. Things were working out as far as I was concerned. The girl didn't try to come on to me and was taking care of business in the day time. I would go to work and come home and talk to Shorty, talk to Girl Girl get some work done, see what she was doing for the company she was supposed to be networking. I noticed that she was not for filling her end of the bargain so I told Shorty to go in there with her and help her out. Make sure she was on her job. I should have never did that because one day Girl Girl asked nicely could she talk to me really softly. When I got around to it she sat in that room and told me "you don't know what she does to me in here while you're gone" she didn't want to get into detail but she burst out in tears. "Nobody ever talked like that to me treated me the way she does, I can't stay here anymore"

The bad thing is I was relieved even though I felt bad. I gave her a care package and took her to the train.

Business as usual. I started going harder; I sold a painting for 45 thousand dollars. That was the most I ever got for a painting. I ran home to tell Shorty. I said- "this is our new beginning. I can't turn back for the things I did or the things you did but it's about what we do now". On New Year's Eve we went to a hotel with the family had some wine and celebrated another year.

I know it was naive for me to think we were going to go up. The money coming in was only a distraction. I noticed that she stopped beefing with me so much. It seemed like she wanted to say some shit but thought better of it and tighten her lips like she had a muzzle on. I didn't care it was our time to come up, she will see now. I was not vaguely interested in any other woman. It was time to really do the shit; she could see now we had something of value. I saw that she was looking at me with squinted eyes. I had my first venue. We did a lot with the R&B stations to promote the art show. Not so many people came out, I expected more. When she seen that it wasn't what I expected it to be she said "I told you. You should have listened to me."

I set up my camera to video record her one day. I wanted to prove how I would try to have a positive conversation and she would immediately turn it into something negative. I wanted every facial expression, every word and every action. Problem was she was hyper vigilant and she noticed the camera as soon as she sat down to speak, but pretended like she didn't see it. Once I asked her a question she said "I don't want to respond because you will just beat me, you always beating on me." I jumped out of my chair and slapped her while the camera was running and said "Like that huh?"

"Yeah like that. You are nothing but a woman beater."

I smacked her again then said "You are not a woman - your a bitch." She turned it all around on me and I lost my self-control. It's funny how you know that domestic violence can put you away for a long time; especially after OJ Simson supposedly killed that white girl, but in the heat of the moment you cannot control yourself. DV laws were ridiculously mild prior to OJ but after he won that case white America was so angry and her father went on a personal crusade for harsh laws against domestic violence, so now if you even breathe on a woman too hard you can go up the river for 5 or more years; and women know it too. Many of them play on that fact and create unnecessary issues.

When you hear about domestic violence all you can do is think of some innocent vulnerable woman being beaten by some evil controlling and manipulating man. You do not naturally think or question how did a love affair turn violent? At some point it had to be good otherwise a couple would not have got together in the first place. Everybody knows or have heard "It takes two to tango." But we do not think about that in domestic issues often. We don't ask ourselves "What part did the woman play in creating a volatile situation or environment?" It usually all falls on the man - the abusive man. So this is my confessions of an abusive man. But I'm not just going to allow you to believe that I am the only one at fault for the problems that led up to violence. Hell no! I will not say that I was correct in resorting to violence, but the way I feel is we were equally responsible. In fact to be totally honest I believe that she was more so responsible because she was the provocateur.

Later on she told me that she seen the recorder on and she was tired of me trying to record her and I guess that is why she began her "You always beating on me" act. It pressed my buttons when she said that; she knew it. She knew how to press my buttons with the slightest of ease; and with all of the knowledge respect I had for women the anger and the heat of the moment over-rided my self-control. Not something I was proud of; in my opinion - she was winning.

I sat in my home office in the dark most days, smoking weed and watching videos on the internet. One day I found a video on Def Jam Poetry. A poet and artist named Black Ice. I loved all of his work and watched him whenever I was in a fucked up mood. I even called her in to watch his videos;

especially one called "The lone souljah."

She started work. She spent wild hours because her schedule was all over the place. I caught 4 traffic tickets driving her to work or rushing to pick her up. One night she was out all night. Another time she claimed she had to work but told me to come pick her up way before her shift was to end, she said they let her go early or some bullshit all I remember truthfully is something was strange about that day. I wanted to have sex but she was trying to turn me off- I ignored her. We had sex and I could smell a strong sent of condom coming out of her pussy. So much that I wiped my dick to smell the wetness and sure nuff. I know what condoms smell like and I did not use them with her. I was turned off immediately and I pretended to nut and got out of her.

One day after she got in from work we had an issue. I had been watching the children, it was a weekend I remember and it was somewhat early, I remember it being bright outside maybe the middle of the day. For some reason I was looking through her purse. I think I was actually looking for the garage key because she had a habit of keeping it in her purse, even though she did not drive. Nana had the spare garage key so I needed the one she had. When she seen me looking through her purse she had a fit. She started questioning me and yelling "What you doing looking in my purse!" She tried to take it from me and I snatched it away.

She walked off and started crying. What made me so irate is she felt that she had every right to search through my clothes, my phone, my Face Book messages, my office - everything; but I did not have a right to search through hers. What's worst is she searched through my things when I was not around so I could not confront her about it. I was not doing that; I was not looking for anything incriminating. Thinking back now; maybe I should have because her response stopped me from looking any further; now my attention was on her. She probably did that to distract me from something she was hiding.

I could not believe her audacity. I tossed her purse on the couch and followed her. "Your crying?" I asked. "Are you serious? After all the shit you've done to me, your crying because I'm looking in your purse?"

"You don't have the right to look through my purse, your the one with the history, your the cheater." I smacked her; not hard but one to show her that I was disgusted, then I went into my office, locked the door and smoked.

I listened to Tupac a lot, he was my favorite artist, and one day this song comes on titled "Can you get away?" It's about a woman in an abusive relationship and Tupac as the Knight in shining armor wants to save her from this creep. I use to love the song before I met her. Now the song made me feel pangs of guilt and misunderstood at the same time. When the song came on while we were in the car she yelled "Turn it up!" and nodded her head to the beat as if she could relate to the story. She was the victim in all of this. I didn't feel like she was the victim at all; I felt like I was the victim or at the very least we both were. But still I felt a horrible wave of shame come over me after hearing the song.

I figured that we needed God in our lives and so I got the Bible out and sat the family down. We all read passages- me, her and Lil Man. The babies fidgeted around but they were more still than usual. This did not help any. I was baffled at how quick she was to entertain nonsense than she was to build on anything positive. Even the bible. I am not even religious so I was doing this for us. That didn't work, I asked her to go with me to see a counselor, and I even took off work to take her to the office. We signed up but when I use to ask her about an appointment she told me there wasn't "nothing" wrong with her and she was "not going to see no counselor"

Chapter 16

I told her one day to listen to this song, it was called "at your best" by Aaliyah. I was hoping it would let her know how I felt about her. She listened but she never said anything, she didn't smile nothing. She just nodded her head then went to finish what she was doing.

It had been years now of her harping on me for networking on the internet. By this time she has all of my passwords to everything. My email, Myspace, Facebook, Tagged, YouTube, Black Planet- everything. She investigates them every day and she gives me shit over what somebody might say or a comment. Then one day I said "hold on you have a MySpace, Face book, Black Planet account, let me have your passwords"- she never gave them to me.

She was quick to tell me that what I was doing would never work, I told her to come up with some ideas, she never did. But what was she doing on the internet? Not business, I know that for damn sure. Even if she was only socializing I had more of a reason to have profiles than she and I didn't follow behind her or argue with her about having her own.

We use to go to the drive in movie theatre all the time, it was the only way we could enjoy the movie and know for sure that our children weren't spoiling it for other people- my kids were all over the place with it. That was all her doing she tried to be vindictive with me after I told her that she wouldn't be getting "hand happy with those two" she decided that she would be their friend their buddy their pal, just to spite me. She would baby them right after I discipline them for doing something wrong. She would not reaffirm by telling them they "could not do that" she would just grab them and hug them and tell them "daddy is just mean" she realized that she made a vital mistake when she noticed she could not control them anywhere. They did not listen because in their little brains they were on the same level as mommy; they were "friends"

I never knew that it truly existed but I believe that she had "Penis Envy." I noticed her jealousy with the way the kids reacted to me and respected me. She did not like that, it was written all over her face. If she told them to stop running in the house or stop playing - they would ignore her. She would have to yell several times; I only had to say it once. She felt they did not respect her because she could not "discipline [her] own children." Meaning beat them like she beat Lil Man. I made it quite clear that if she hit them - I hit her - period.

I did not mind if she spanked them for something that they did wrong, but like I said she would not get "Hand Happy" with them. She also felt that they did not respect her because I was "abusive" to her. I guess she would have preferred that they did not respect me; she wanted me to accept the way she treated and spoke to me without protest and surly the children would have followed her lead. I am sure that there are men that live like that; with their woman and children disrespecting them; I seen it in my hood; but I am not built for that type of affliction. I'm not having it.

I remember times when she tried to justify her child abuse and turn me against her own son. At times he would hit the children because he was angry about something that she did to him and she would beat him then tell me "You see, that's why," but at those times I really felt that she was a piece of shit, but I didn't say it.

When I came home from work both my children would run up to me yelling "Daddy!" and grab on to my legs; I would walk into my office with one on each leg, clinging on to me, it's as if they thought it was a ride in an amusement park. That was the best part of the day for me - the best part of my life. Sometimes she would be so jealous and angry when they did that that you could see the steam coming from her head. I think that she just hated the fact that I got such an abundant welcoming from them that she did not get. The truth was I was out all day; so they had time to miss me, while she was with them all day. It did not mean that they cherished me more so than they did her. Everything was a competition for her.

Now in order to get them to listen she will have to beat them and I was not going for it. She hated me for that. She said that she can't discipline her own kids. In my mind I said she will not do to these two what she did to Lil Man at all ever period. Not only she was "hand happy" with him, she also didn't allow him to do anything, I mean like for years. I brought him a play station when it came out and he rarely ever got to play it. He was always being sent to his room. He spent more time in there than anywhere in the house, so much that it didn't bother him no more to be stuck in the room. Going outside was strictly for bidden, he had to go around her and ask me first just to see the light of day. He got in trouble for that too.

When she beat him now she not only puts hands but she drags him to his room and forbid him to come out and to shut up. When he continues to cry she goes inside and gives him some more.

"It is untrue that all batterers have antisocial personality traits or that they will be violent in all their relationships. Even in abusive relationships the batterer can be caring, can be a loving person and the relationship can improve. But in order to elicit change there must be a drastic change of events or intervention.

*The majority of domestic victims do not realize that there is a cycle of violence, it is not a random isolated event - there is a pattern. As the cycle of violence continues, the assaults and injuries become more frequent and damaging." -**PTSD Raymond***

Flannery PhD.

One morning, just before it was time for me to drive to work, we got into a really bad argument that seemed to come out of nowhere, so I told her to "Get out!" I was just making a toothless threat, I didn't expect her to leave early in the morning and I had to go to work, I could not take off and someone had to watch the children. But she called my bluff and was out the door and out of sight before I could do anything. I drove around the neighborhood to find her; she could not have gotten very far on foot; but she was nowhere to be found. I had to call in late (to a supervisor who was tired of my relationship problems) and ran the children over to Nanas house. She was missing the entire day. When she returned she said that she was at the library. Yeah. Right.

One day I had to go to court. I took off work. She went with me. Her and my two Lil Ones. When we got back in the house I don't know what started the argument, I just know I smacked her she kept egging me on saying "come on beat me like you always do" I hated to hear that and it thru me into a rage, because I never wanted to hit her to begin with, I always came to talk it out. I tried to drop kick her for saying it and my children were watching.

She never tried to diffuse the situation not even when it was heated, she always had to be hard. She always had to say something to make it worst. I called the police and handed her the phone. She never called the police when shit got out of hand. I felt like I was not in control of myself with her and since she wouldn't do it- I did.

When she seen that I really dialed the police station she hung up the phone on the officer. I walked away into my room and started smoking trees. Within 15 minutes there was a knock at my door. The police came to my home to see if everything was okay. She lied to them. They asked me to step outside. This was her opportunity to tell them that she was being "abused" I spoke to the male officer she spoke to the female officer. I was very standoffish with the officer and told him "I ain't telling you shit" he was being very polite to me though. That is what changed my attitude toward him. I told him that me and my wife were having problems and I called them. She told them we were just arguing so they took down some notes and left.

Why hadn't she told them? She wanted things to stay the way they were. I was suffering more than she. I didn't want to be put in jail so I would not tell them that I hit her. I wanted her to tell them, I was not going to tell on myself. I would have done that with a counselor because I felt that a counselor would have helped the situation for us both, but the police would just put me away.

There was no winning with her. She would not go to the

counselor, she would not talk to me, she would not even tell the police; I'd just had to deal with the way things were even though I was dying inside. I called Nana over one day because I had a plan to get out. I did not ever intend to pay this woman child support and I did not trust her to raise my children without my stark observation. At the same time I could not take care of my children on my own and she did not have money or a job or a home, so she could not take care of them either.

My plan was simple; we leave the children with Nana until we both get on our feet, whoever gets established first and can provide the kids with security - that parent takes possession of the kids. Of course I already had a house and a job, but I had the need to start new. I sat them both down and explained my plan, when Nana agreed to mind the children for us - that's when Nana got to witness a small dose of her true personality. She flipped on Nana and accused Nana of taking my side because "that's your family."

The truth is that Nana did not take anyone's side. She disagreed with me on a lot of issues concerning her and she disagreed with her on some of her behavior. But the thing about Nana is she always tried to keep the peace, she was soft spoken and always reliable for both of us. She was angry because she felt that Nana should have not dared to agree to take custody of the children because she's a woman - she's a mother. She felt Nana would side with her because Nana is a woman and mother herself. But Nana was not thinking about the woman's code, she was worried about the children's welfare. I'm sure Nana did not want the responsibility of raising our children, she had adult children and grandchildren.

Nana and her argued a bit as Nana attempted to tell her that she was agreeing to do it for the kids benefit. Shorty did not care, if you did not share her opinion or take her side - you were the enemy. Nana agreed that we were not good for each other.

A few months later Nana had a visitor, a pretty Red Bone girl. When I met her I knew she was trouble. She was easy to talk to, she smoked weed and she had done some time in prison – we had a lot in common. On our second meeting I learned that she was a freak. She wanted me to take pictures of her to put on the internet. For some internet dating service; I agreed. When she came over I found out that she wanted to take butt ass naked flicts. I was surprised but I was with it. She told me that she could make money on the site and she would pay me. The problem was although she was pretty; she dressed like a tomboy; she didn't even own sexy lingerie. I decided to allow her to borrow my wife's underwear for the photo shoot; I reasoned that Shorty didn't wear sexy underwear for me no way unless I practically begged her to. Besides she would never find out anyway.

How silly of me to believe that she would never find out. While I was at work she went scrolling through my photos and found all the pictures of Red Bone with all her lingerie on. She called Nana "hysterical" and emailed Nana the naked flics. If I said that I felt bad – I would be lying; I just felt bad that I got caught.

I felt bad that it was someone that Nana knew and I felt bad that she could use the situation to justify why we did not get along and Nana would believe her. Other than that – I did not care. I felt that she earned whatever bullshit I could do. I only attempted to explain to her because I wanted peace in my house hold. Whenever I tried to talk to her about anything it didn't make one bit of a difference. I tried to tell her if she stopped treating me the way she did I would stop responding to it.

It burns me up inside every time and I talk to her about it. She listens but doesn't say a word. At this point I am in a daze about the whole thing. I don't know if I was the cause or she, I just want the madness to be over. I tell her to take a bath and meet me in the guest room- naked. I got her in there and told her to get on her knees. She started to protest, she had long before then stopped sucking my dick, but that's not what I wanted. I got on the floor with her naked bowed my head and prayed that God forgive us and guide us. I told her Adam and Eve who is our mother and father had to address God naked and when they didn't he noticed. So naked must be the proper way to address God. That didn't help our marriage one bit.

I became so bitter that I would slap her every time she said something disrespectful out of her mouth; and that was quite often. It was principal now. In the beginning it took several degrading or disrespectful statements to get me to the point where I would put hands; now, from the slightest provocation – I would go off.

I was like a ticking time bomb. In fact; I started to look for a reason. I would start a conversation with her knowing that she would say something offensive – then smack her face. All the remorse or shame I had completely deteriorated; now I believed that she deserved everything she got; in fact she earned it.

I felt like I had been deceived from day one; that she never intended on trying to make things work. That she used me as a sperm donor and intended on separating so she could get custody of the kids and have me pay child support. There's a bunch of women that get pregnant for their own ulterior motives; and the man is the sucker that got hooked. Nobody wants to be played for a fool; and when you play with a person's emotions it can become a very dangerous situation.

I was driving when a song came on the radio, I turned it up so I could hear the words, it was called "I love the way you lie" by Eminem ft. Rihanna.

I started to get the idea that it was over between us when I tried to talk to her but she would sit still looking blank and waiting until I was finished talking to walk away. It made me hate her so much that one day I decided I wanted some payback. I don't remember what the issue was that ignited it but I decided to take her for a ride; a rough ride.

I told her to get in the car. She got in and I drove off and left the kids in the house unattended. I drove to a spot that no one could hear her. Once she said something I reached over and slapped her – hard. I parked the car on a dark road and began to beat her. Not the usual slap out of frustration; I was really beating her now and I did not care.

She tried to escape. When she attempted to get out of the car, I locked the car doors and beat her some more. She began to yell and I yelled with her. "Nobody's going to hear you you stinking bitch; I should kill you."

As I started driving she attempted to unlock the doors so she could jump out but I had control of the locks on the driver's side. I was irate and out of control because I knew it was over after all that I invested; I just didn't know how it would end. After some time passed, once again I rocked myself to sleep.

I had to find a way to make her understand, I looked on the internet on *Emotional Abuse*. It had everything in there that I was going thru with her and the way people respond. I admit I respond a bit extra but I wanted to see a family counselor about my anger and her behavior, but she failed to keep up with the dates I signed up for. I signed us up on two separate occasions, even took off of work to do it. How many street dudes you know telling his wife they need to go to counseling? How many women you know that would say "no" to that?

> *"Even though there are no broken bones or bruises, emotional/verbal abuse can cause equally long-term psychological scars. In fact this can be worst because it is not apparent and the wounds perpetuates itself in the victims own mind."*

I believed that I was a victim of mental, emotional and verbal abuse. I believed that the mental abuse was worse than physical abuse because mental abuse cannot be seen with the naked eye and takes much longer to heal. After while I just wanted the pain to be over. I was tired of fighting. I was tired of disagreeing, I was tired of being lonely in a house full of people. Still I could not leave her; I did not have the will power to leave.

I was so elated to see on line what I was trying to explain to her all the time, I was sure she would believe that what I was saying was real. I called her to come into my office and sit down. I said "I found something I want you and I to read together," I began reading:

> Does your girlfriend or wife yell, scream, and swear at you? Do you feel like you can't talk to anyone about your relationship because they just wouldn't understand? Is your relationship making you feel like you're slowly going crazy?
>
> If so, you're probably involved with a woman who is an emotionally abusive bully. Most men don't want to admit that they're in an abusive relationship. They describe the relationship and their girlfriend/wife using other terms like crazy, emotional, controlling, bossy, domineering, constant conflict, or volatile. If you use words like this to describe your relationship, odds are you're being emotionally abused.
>
> Do you recognize any of the following behaviors?
>
> **1) Bullying** – *If she doesn't get her way, there's hell to pay.* She wants to control you and resorts to emotional intimidation to do it. She uses verbal assaults and threats in order to get you to do what she wants. It makes her feel powerful to make you feel bad. People with a **Narcissistic Personality** are often bullies.
>
> *Result*: You lose your self-respect and feel outnumbered, sad, and alone. You develop a case of **Stockholm Syndrome**, in which you identify with the aggressor and actually defend her behavior to others.
>
> **2) Unreasonable Expectations** – No matter how hard you try and how much you give, it's never enough. She

expects you to drop whatever you're doing and attend to her needs. No matter the inconvenience, she comes first. She has an endless list of demands that no one mere mortal could ever fulfill. Common complaints include: You're not romantic enough, you don't spend enough time with me, you're not sensitive enough, you're not smart enough to figure out my needs, you're not making enough money, you're not FILL IN THE BLANK enough. Basically, you're not enough, because there's no pleasing this woman. *No one will ever be enough for her, so don't take it to heart.*

Result: You're constantly criticized because you're not able to meet her needs and experience a sense of **Learned Helplessness**. You feel powerless and defeated because she puts you in "no win" situations.

3) Verbal Attacks – This is self-explanatory. She employs schoolyard name calling, psycho pathological epithets (e.g., armed with a superficial knowledge of psychology she uses diagnostic terms like labile, paranoid, narcissistic, etc. to make it appear that she knowledgeable in psychological disorders, when along with back alley insults; she is only using these terms to put you down and insult your intelligence as well), criticizing, threatening, screaming, cursing, sarcasm, humiliation, exaggerating your flaws, and making fun of you in front of others, including your children and other people she's not intimidated by. *Verbal Assault* is another form of bullying, and bullies only act like this in front of those whom they don't fear or people who let them get away with their bad behavior.

4) Gas Lighting – "I didn't do that. I didn't say that. I don't know what you're talking about. It wasn't that bad. You're imagining things. Stop making things up." If the woman you're involved with is prone to **Borderline or Narcissistic rage episodes**, in which she spirals into a possessed ranting fit, she may well not remember things she said and done. However, don't doubt your perception and memory of events. They happened and they are "that bad."

Result: Her gas lighting behavior may cause you to doubt your own sanity or the chain of events that you experienced. It's crazy making behavior that leaves you feeling confused, bewildered, and helpless.

5) Unpredictable Responses – She reacts differently to you on different days or at different times. This is another Borderline characteristic. For example, on Monday its okay for you to Email or Text work related messages on your smart phone, in her presence. On Wednesday, the same behavior is considered disrespectful, inappropriate, or insensitive. She may say something like "You don't have no consideration for my feelings, your selfish, you only think about yourself, since you care more about your work than anything else – than leave me alone." By Friday its okay for you to send or respond to Emails or Texts again. Telling you one day that something is alright and the next day it is not; is *emotionally abusive* behavior. It's like walking through a landmine in which the mines shift location.

Result: You're constantly on edge, walking on eggshells, and not knowing when she is going to blow up or what she is going to blow up for. This makes you constantly on guard, anticipating but trying to avoid attack. This is a Trauma Response. You're being traumatized by her behavior. Because you cannot predict her responses, you become hyper vigilant to any change in her mood or potential outburst, which leaves you in a perpetual state of anxiety and possibly fear. It's a healthy sign to be afraid of this behavior men. It's scary. Do not feel ashamed to admit it.

6) Constant Chaos – She's addicted to conflict. She gets a charge from the adrenaline and drama. She may deliberately start arguments and conflict as a way to avoid intimacy or being called on her shenanigans. She may also pick fights to keep you engaged or as a way to get you to react to her with hostility, so that she can accuse you of being abusive and she can be the victim later on. This maneuver is a defense mechanism called **Projective Identification**.

Result: You become emotionally punch drunk. You're left feeling dazed and confused, not knowing which end is up. This is highly stressful because it also requires you to be hyper vigilant and in a constant state of defense for incoming attacks.

7) Emotional Blackmail – She threatens to abandon you, to end the relationship, or give you the cold shoulder if you don't play by her rules. She plays on your fears, vulnerabilities, weaknesses, shame, values, sympathy, compassion, and any other "buttons" to control you and get what she wants.

Result: You feel manipulated, used and controlled.

8) Rejection – She ignores you, won't look at you when you're in the same room, gives you the cold shoulder, withholds affection, withholds sex, declines or puts down your ideas, invitations, suggestions, and pushes you away when you try to be close. After she pushes you as hard and as far away as she can, she'll try to be affectionate with you. You're still hurting from her previous rebuff or attack and do not respond. Then she accuses you of being cold and rejecting, which she'll use as an excuse to push you away again in the future.

Result: You feel undesirable, unwanted, unlovable. You believe no one else would want you and cling to this abusive woman, grateful for whatever scraps of infrequent affection she shows you.

9) Withholding Affection and Sex – This is another form of rejection and emotional blackmail. It's not just about sex, it's about withholding physical, psychological, and emotional nurturing. It includes a lack of interest in what's important to you – your job, family, friends, hobbies, activities and being uninvolved, emotionally detached or shut down with you.

Result: You have a transactional relationship in which you have to perform tasks, buy her things, "be nice to her," or give into her demands in order to receive love and affection from her. You do not feel loved and appreciated for who you are, but for what you do for her or purchase for her.

10) Isolating – She demands or acts in ways that cause you to distance yourself from your family, friends, or anyone that would be concerned for your well-being or a source of support. This typically involves verbally trashing your friends and family, being overtly hostile to your family and friends, or acting out and starting arguments in front of others to make it as unpleasant as possible for them to be around the two of you.

Result: This makes you completely dependent upon her. She takes away your outside sources of support and/or controls the amount of interaction you have with them. You're left feeling trapped and alone, afraid to tell anyone what really goes on in your relationship because you don't think they'll believe you. You don't have to accept *Emotional Abuse* in your relationship. You can get help or you can end it. Most *Emotionally Abusive* women don't want help. They don't think they need it. They are the professional victims, bullies, narcissists, and borderlines. They're abusive personality types and don't know any other way to act in relationships.

That was exactly how I felt, she was just looking straight as if she was waiting for the point, I continued. This was good she always did this and I wanted her to hear it from another source other than me. Many days and nights I called to talk to her and spent hours trying to explain what I was feeling. This was great. I read:

Denying

- Denying a person's emotional needs, especially when they feel that need the most, and done with the intent of hurting, punishing or humiliating.
- The other person may deny that certain events occurred or that certain things were said. Confronts the abuser about an incident of name calling, the abuser may insist, "I never said that," "I don't know what you're talking about," etc. You know differently.
- The other person may deny your perceptions, memory and very sanity.
- Withholding is another form of denying. Withholding includes refusing to listen, refusing to communicate, and emotionally withdrawing as punishment. This is sometimes called "The Silent Treatment."
- When the abuser disallows and overrules any viewpoints, perceptions or feeling which differ from their own.
- Denying can be particularly damaging. In addition to lowering self-esteem and creating conflict, the invalidation of reality, feelings, and experiences can eventually lead you to question and mistrust your own perceptions and emotional experience.
- Denying and other forms of emotional abuse can cause you to lose confidence in your most valuable survival tool – your own mind.

She sat there and acts like I was saying nothing. I began to wonder was she listening at all. I got excited about the next one and began to read with much more excitement. This was good stuff and I needed her open her eyes and notice what she was doing and the affects that it has on me. I was in a good mood I smiled and started reading with more energy:

Dominating

- Someone wants to control your every action. They want to have their own way, and resort to threats to get it.

  When you allow someone else to dominate you, you can lose respect for yourself.

She had to know that she did that. That was plain to see. But she never acknowledged it, she said nothing, I kept reading, something was going to reach her. I didn't know then what I expected from her, by now my mind was mush. I really wanted her to say "Baby is that what you were feeling? I'm sorry I put you thru that. I'm sorry I put us all thru that. Can you ever forgive me?" I would have, I already did forgive her, but I was only being delusional, she never had before and wouldn't now.

Was she seeing the similarities in our relationship? This is what went on in our home every day; this knowledge has to change things because we could now point a finger at it. I read some more:

Understanding Abusive Relationships

No one intends to be in an abusive relationship, but individuals who were verbally abused by a parent or other significant person often find themselves in similar situations as an adult. If a parent tended to define your experiences and emotions, and judge your behaviors, you may not have learned how to set your own standards, develop your own viewpoints and validate your own feeling and perceptions. Consequently, the controlling and defining stance taken by an emotional abuser may feel familiar or even conformable to you, although it is destructive.

Recipients of abuse often struggle with feelings of powerlessness, hurt, fear, and anger. Ironically abusers tend to struggle with these same feelings. Abuser are also likely to have been raised in emotionally abusive environments and they learn to be abusive as a way to cope with their own feelings of powerlessness, hurt, fear, and anger. Consequently, abusers may be attracted to people who see themselves as helpless or who have not learned to value their own feelings, perceptions, or viewpoints. This allows the abuser to feel more secure and in control, and avoid dealing with their own feelings, and self-perceptions.

I didn't want to lose her and she was not being receptive. This was the last thing I would say about it then give her the web address and let her go on her own time. Usually she was on when I was at work. This was the most important cause it gave us instructions:

Basic Needs In Relationships

If you have been involved in Emotionally Abusive relationships, you may not have a clear idea of what a healthy relationship is like.

- The need for good will from the other.
- The need for emotional support.

- The need to be heard by the other and to be responded to with respect and acceptance.
- The need to have your own view, even if others have a different view.
- The need to have your feelings and experience acknowledged as real.
- The need to receive a sincere apology for any jokes or actions you find offensive.
- The need for clear, honest and informative answers to questions about what affects you.
- The need for freedom from accusation, interrogation and blame.
- The need to live free from criticism and judgment.
- The need to have your work and your interests respected.
- The need for encouragement.
- The need for freedom from emotional and physical threat.
- The need for freedom from angry outburst and rage.
- The need for freedom from labels which devalue you.
- The need to be respectfully asked rather than ordered.
- The need to have your final decisions accepted.
- The need for privacy at times.

When I finally stopped reading it was clear to me that she didn't care about anything that I said, like always she was just waiting for me to stop talking.

We spent the money but weren't selling any more paintings for that amount of money. The regular arguments continued. I was not there from that point on. I lived in a daze. What I didn't know then was she was just waiting for an opportunity to strike. Maybe in the back of my mind I always knew she would, I just ignored my rational. I had become good at ignoring my own thoughts to the point of not having any. I was talking about separating a lot now.

I told her she needed time and so did I, away from each other. I wanted to keep the kids and the section 8 until she got a place of her own, then we would share visitation. It was mostly just feeble threats at first but when it didn't work I went to the next level and took her down the section 8 office and took her name off my account so she cold know it was real, but I was wishing that will scare her into changing and come to the table to really deal with the issues that were destroying our family. I knew how vindictive she was but I did it anyway. We still lived together though and were somewhat getting along. Meaning; that we were not at each other's throats. I didn't realize then that I had become just like her, playing songs when I was angry, I would play a song like *"Duce's"* the remix loud, but I really didn't mean it. There was another song I played then cause I liked it, and it was how I felt it was a song called "all I want is you" by Miguel. Without a word she then kidnapped the children and moved to another state.

Chapter 18

I started a YouTube channel called checkavailability442 and put all the songs that reminded me of her on there, I listened to my play list every night and cried my eyes out. I couldn't even think to take care of myself. I was not eating, I felt lost and didn't know where to turn. None of my friends and family wanted anything to do with me now. I was not communicating with them when I was "doing good" and they felt I deserted them in a way. They were not exactly wrong about that they just didn't know why I failed to keep the lines of communication open. I blamed her for that.

I spent months in torment over where she could be. Finally I called on a friend "with connections" to find her. He had an address for me later on that day. I immediately drive to Virginia. I set myself up an apartment. I had to take the money out of my business account because she had cleaned out the joint account. She didn't know that I knew where she was. I drove over there in a rental car and I seen her getting dropped off at her cousins house with another man. That was not as painful as seeing my children get out of the car. I grabbed the door handle then caught myself. One tear dropped from my eye. How could she kidnap the kids and not let me know where they were? How could her heart be so cold? How could she have my children around another man? I started sending her emails. That was the only way I could get a word in before she hung up the phone on me. She let me speak to the children for 1 minute apiece, whenever she felt like it. I spoke to them 3 times this year. She still has not come to me to try and settle things. I figured that she needed time; it was even alright that she slept with another man. I wanted to forgive her and get my family back. I waited.

4-22-11

I sent her some online divorce papers. Really just as a threat, she didn't respond.

From: Him

To: Her

Date: 5-11-11

I lost my phone...I don't know your number so I guess this is it. Bye

----

From: Him

To: Her

Subject:

Date: Thu, 12 May 2011 07:37:48 -0400

Yesterday I was pulled over by the police. This was the 4th time that I have been pulled over- 3rd ticket. They pulled me out of the car, searched me and wanted to take me in. I was thinking if they did you would never know where I was. Nobody I know would know where I was cause I don't know anybody number by heart. Now that I lost my phone I can't even contact my grandmother. My old world is dead and I will not back track to find anyone. Are you happy now? Now that I'm suffering and I have no one to turn to for help are you happy? You should be. You were successful. You destroyed everything about me. You took everything from me that I cared for. You violated our marriage and you deserted me. God will bless you because of the goodness of your heart. I will not humiliate myself any further by contacting you again. It's great to see how much you care for me, thank you for being so good to me, caring for me, concerned for my safety.

God Son

From: Her

To: Him

Subject: RE:

Date: Thu, 12 May 2011 19:46:18 -0500

Stop being angry every time we talk and there would b more communication, my number is. I'm always concerned about ur well being, take care.

From: Him

To: Her

Subject: RE:

Date:

I don't express my anger over the phone with you, but u know that I am upset about the way things went down. I still have no access to my kids or wife, and it's all your decisions. When I didn't have my own then u had an excuse, but now that I do I know for sure that this is all your idea. I never would have guessed that, I would have put my life on it. But anyway I just got in I had one hell of a night. I don't have a phone and I let go of my job. it's too far from where I stay and that day I was stranded I got paranoid, so I'm in limbo now, but anyway you won't believe this but I had dinner with a director of the Monique show and a dude that works for Tyler Perry...he bought a painting...I hope that he likes it enough to mention it to his employer. There also was a girl from LA she was featured in a movie premier today, it was an independent film but she is in the wire. she was feeling me, she kept looking in my face even though I look like a crack head, she hugged me goodbye twice...I told them about you...not the bad shit just I had a wife...I didn't have a phone for them to contact me with, but I gave them my card anyway. I leave my life in God's hands now; I don't have any direction so I am going where God leads me. I can only pray that I am doing what God wants me to do. I will not get another phone for a while so we will not talk for a bit. I'm working on a new job opportunity but this one is closer. I hope that my family is safe and that you all are good. Take care.

From: Him

To: Her

5-12-11

tell my children that I love them, words can express it...tell them that I didn't understand y they loved me, but I will always be with them...they have my face so every time ya'll look in the mirror I will be there. I know life will be hard for ya'll but it is hard for most people. Be strong. Be stronger than me, and take care of one another. Daddy loves you always. Bye my babies

Amiri

This was intended to be my last message to my children. I never said "bye" to my babies, I only said "see you later." I was going to commit suicide. I got really drunk and smoked a lot of weed and cried. When I laid down with the gun in my hand; suddenly my phone started to ring off the hook. It was Nana calling. It was my old homeboy calling. It was my cousin calling.

I believed it was a sign from God and I finally answered the phone. They did not know it; but on that night – they saved my life.

From: Him
To: Her
Subject:
Date: Fri. 20, May 2011 18:55:25

Here's the deal...you need to stop what you are doing. I am okay with the fact that you have moved on with your life. By your total lack of communication I am certain you are with someone else. Granted, I am even dealing with the fact that you are with another man. It is wrong to have my children around another man at this stage of their lives; I would not have done that to you out of respect of your motherhood. I earned respect as a father; I worked 16hrs a day 7 days a week for my children. To make sure they had a roof over their head and food in their stomach. You have no respect for the fact that I am a devote father and I do not run away from my responsibilities as a father. You kidnapped the children for your own motives. You don't answer the phone when I call and you call me when you are around a lot of noise. I know it's because you don't want me to know where you are and you can't talk in front of whoever you are with. This is not making our situation better it is making it worst and from the sign of things that is exactly the way you want it to be. I will ask one time and as humbly as I can- do not try to deceive me anymore.

I will not ask you about where you are staying and I will not tell you where I am staying. You have destroyed any trust between us. If somebody wants to see me- just let me know, I will meet anybody anywhere at any time. My patients with you is at an end, I have tried to see the positive in all of this, but now I see you are manipulating me, and taking my kindness and concern as a weakness and a upper hand. I did my best, that was not enough, but do not try and manipulate me, it is transparent. You don't have to say two words to me if that is what you are trying, just let me speak to my kids every week and I'm good. If you don't want to meet up with me and try to settle things, I don't want to talk to you at all. Period. Keep biding time and it will be your loss. I will not get with you when you "get your shit together" where ever you are it must be better than what I had to offer you as a husband, so stay there. All I want from you now, all that you can offer me is communication with my children. I want to speak to them and I want to see them.

You can choose the place, but not the time because my schedule is crazy now days. You can offer a time and I will let you know if I could make it or not. We can establish a pick up and drop off spot, you can have a police escort if you want beings that all of a sudden you are "so scared" of me. In fact I think that would be the best idea, this way I can't say that you were not allowing me the right I have as a father to see and speak to my children. I don't care all I care about is reconnecting with my little ones. If you are not willing to do these things- don't bother contacting me again. When the welfare contacts me for child support then all the laundry will be out in the open and things will change for you. I prefer that we work it out instead, but you can have it your way as always. Okay.

Tell my children that I love them and I will see them soon.

My cousin came to visit me and I really needed her mentally. I was emotionally sick and her presence alone sustained me. It gave me the opportunity to get out of my own head. Random urges to kill myself kept penetrating my thoughts. I was saved twice by divine intervention. In order to get out of the house and try to keep my thoughts off Her and my kids I would drive around and listen to music. There was this one song by Jada Kiss called "Lil Brah" that I played repeatedly; it helped to encourage me but it made me cry. I would listen to that song while driving aimlessly with blurry eyes; it helped along with the cigarettes and weed.

From: Her

To: Him
Subject: RE
Date: Sat, 21, May 2011 08:59:05

Stop worrying about me being with another man because that is not the case, furthermore I have no questions and/or concerns about who you are with. For the last time I am just trying to get myself together. The kids will continue to call you twice a week. My hesitance with meeting with you is because you go back and forth with being alright with the situation as it is and being angry, never know which one I am going to get. When we are in the car with you, no one but you knows the destination, if you're going to let us etc. Anyway the point is I don't want to beef with you or for you to be angry with me, we will all see each other soon enough.

From: Him

To: Her

Why r u lying "twice a week" I haven't heard from u twice a month. Not even once a month. You won't answer the phone if u know it's me. If u "don't care" who I'm with-there's no need for us 2 be married. I care, I'm offended and I don't believe u. Why all the secrecy? You don't answer any of my text, haven't let me see or speak to the children for months at a time and to top it all off I don't know where my children are. Like always u do something and expect me not to react. You would b angry if I took the kids and u did not know where they were. I never was "alright" with what you have done I only tried to keep it civil and u don't respond to that either. You don't have to get in the car Shorty at all, just drop the kids off.

From: Him

To: Her

I have been thinking about us. From start to finish. We made a mess of all this. I really did some fucked up shit to you and I still haven't really understood what and how it affected you. It was impulsive to my defense. I was reacting from you but I know that it was too much. I didn't mean to hurt you, or harm your heart. I didn't know what I was doing. I was out of my mind, and you put me there. I failed to use my brain at some point. The stress with us not working was too much for me. I invested everything on it. If you think about it you will see, that I made you my life. You never seen it and I didn't want you to run all over me so I had to defend myself. The majority of the time I was innocent for what you were accusing me of and it wore me out baby. I couldn't talk to you didn't listen to anything once you got an idea in your head that was it. There was nothing that could change it. You were abusing me, why can't you see that. I fell off. I stopped thinking for myself I started smoking like it was going out of style, hoping one day you would stop me. Tell me to stop. Stop making me feel like smoking. I can't believe some of the things we did to each other looking back now. I apologize for my part. I always take my blame you never take yours. If you did we probably could have prevented us from destroying our love. I was sleep walking though baby, my head in the cloud made the easier not to pay attention to what was happening. I didn't want it to be so I ignored it hoping it would go away on its own, that didn't work I talked to you- you did not respond. The only way was like this to you I can see. You never tried to make it better baby even when I was trying. You are right to move on, I just don't want you to because I know that we could have done better. But it's a two way street, one person can't do it alone when it takes two. You left that burden on me and you weren't trying to come to a middle ground. You just didn't want this. You didn't ever give it a shot though, that is what bugs me out. If you tried we would have had a mighty love. I know it. Even when we were at each other's throats look at what we accomplished. I can't minimize your part, I always say you only did what I asked you to do, but the bottom line is you did it and that is where I went wrong taking that for granted. If we got along we would have had anything we wanted. But we spent too much time and energy in not getting along. I brought that to the light and you still didn't want or try to change our lives together. That drove me crazy in my mind. I wanted us to work. I seen the potential. But I wasn't going to be no push over or punk for you. You would never respect me if I did. The price was too heavy to pay. I did some wild shit but I really didn't know what I was doing. I was there but I was not there at all. You are the best thing that happened to me, there I said it. I'm not dead that don't make me less than a man to admit. I don't care what people think of me anymore, nobody cares anyway so their opinion of me means less to me that old dirty gum stuck to the ground. I am afraid to know what you are doing. I can't understand how u could live without me, that is not the case for me. I can't go a few hours without thinking about you. It's been like that from the day I walked into your life. I was always with you or on the phone with you where ever I was; I kept you and thoughts of you with me. My torch. My reason. I hope that you can see with my eyes as is see through yours. I love you

From: Her
To: Him
Subject: RE
Date: Wed, 25, May 2011 10:15:16

Apparently yesterday I was suppose to add minutes to my phone, when I woke up I couldn't use it that's how I found out. Moving on, your words touched me immensely. I'll always love and have a soft spot for you. When you're nice, you make me feel like I'm floating but I know the ugly parts of you and that's hard to ignore. One min I think we're making progress being friends again then you send me a text talking about you want custody of the kids? Even though you've done a lot to me that I won't get into detail about in an email I still feel the need to look out and protect you. You know that about me and sometimes take advantage of it.

From: Him

To: Her

You know that I say what I think, even if it never materializes. I was just thinking of all the shit. I can't talk about everything over this key board, that's why I am so upset that you don't even try to communicate so we can talk about it get it out in the open and heal the wounds we caused each other. Not even to get together, but because we didn't mean to treat each other that way. I know that I didn't. I really went mad over this shit. I was really sleepwalking I couldn't think past our problems and it had a deep seeded affect on my mind and heart. You never communicated with me you chose to tell your friends that were across the world instead of working on your home at home. That didn't make sense to me and every day you did it made me lose confidence in you, and that fucked me up because you were it. Even if I did slip and slide off one day I knew there would be no other woman for me. You were for life. That's why when I noticed that you were determined to destroy our relationship, I could not accept it. I could not accept you talking down to me everyday cursing at me everyday doing little nasty things like tossing my food in front of me. I don't let people talk to me in any kind of way, you know that. I can't even sleep if I think someone tried to play me. You can imagine my sleeping habits now. You talked dirty and down to me every day. I knew that we were over. The thing was though, that you were like that from the beginning. Protect me??? You know that I protect you. I am over protective of you. That's why not knowing where you are hurts because I can't do my job. What if you need me? You know while I have the potential I will not hurt you. yes I'm mad I am in a rage in fact, what you did was and is still devastating but I still I worry that I won't get there in time if you need me. I won't know where to go or who to see. You know I will not bother you; I will only come when I have to but you do this? That means one of two things maybe both you don't want me to know where you are because you are involved with another man and you don't want me to disturb that and because you want to hurt me to my heart and soul. You were successful if that makes you feel better.

From: Him

To: Her

We can make progress at being friends when you are up front with me Shorty. You don't have to tell me where you are staying right now, but you do need to let me know what you want to happen from all of this. I don't see any good in it. You need to be straight forward with me about what you want what you are doing what you want to happen for you. You need to let me know if I am in that picture, be forth coming. Which is something that you have failed to do our whole relationship. I had to find out your real feelings and intentions by stumbling into letters you wrote yourself. You can't try to deceive me on one hand then try to say you are working on a friendship with me. You haven't called, how is that working on a friendship? You haven't contacted me in any way but you are working on a friendship? The 3 times you allowed the kids to call you made sure it was brief and you did not get on the phone, that is working on a friendship with me? You have to actually do something to claim that you are "working" on something.

From: Her
To: Him
Subject: RE
Date: Thu, 26, May 2011 05:02:45

I just got finished watching a movie called The Adjustment Bureau, watch it.

From: Her
To: Him
Date: May 27 3:44pm

We've been through a lot, please do not make me feel like I'm being selfish or trying to hurt you because I am not. I need this time to heal. My heart is hurting thinking about you being out there and not having. Feel free to call me

Amiri

That was the last email I got from her and she still never answered my calls even after saying "feel free" to call.

Chapter 19

I would sing a song called "Diamond in the rough" by Jaheim in my room at the top of my lungs wishing she somehow could hear my soul crying out to her. She never did.

I thought "abuse" was like my father; slapping my mother around because he wanted or needed money for drugs. I thoughts "abuse" was the alcoholic father we seen on TV shows that comes home drunk and slaps his wife around because he was down on his luck. I thought "abuse" was an insecure man wanting to blame his problems, bad luck or inadequacies on his weaker wife or his vulnerable children.

I thought "abuse" was a sick person that felt inferior and weak in life and wanted to control the only people that he could – his only family. But abuse is control; I was none of those other things but I did want to control my wife. I wanted her to control her attitude and behavior, and I wanted some form of control over her thoughts and actions as well; not in a bad way though. I suppose that makes me abusive as well but not in the sense that I recognized to be abuse.

I wanted my wife to educate herself on Black history and Black Nationalism. When she did not take an interest; I did not get mad and beat her for it; but it did disappoint me; in fact it disgusted me to a certain extent; but that did not result in violence. I wanted my wife to be more responsible about how she spent money; and I took control over what she could and could not spend. I know that she hated that because she enjoyed spending money...but my belief is if we saved more, we could have more of a future. I wanted to invest in business until it had a life of its own, she wanted to spend any extra money on material things that depreciate over time like clothing, appliances and furniture. I wanted to break her out of that type of thinking completely. I wanted her to be more business orientated. I believe that if you have two dollars, make four before you spend two. This made her absolutely and completely unhappy. I believe that my control tactics were more in the line of teaching, but she believed that I just wanted to "control" her.

I did not think I was "abusive" in the sense that I wanted my wife to know how to shoot. I took her to the shooting range so she could learn; she hated me for that too. But I did it just incase she had to protect herself and the family. I did not think that the "abusive man" would want to teach the "victim" how to protect themselves. She did not want to learn how to shoot; I was "forcing" her to do that too.

I did end up forcing her to do things; but not under the threat that I would beat her if she did not. I felt like she did when I was living in her apartment "You live here; so your going to do something." It was more than just her living with me, I was providing everything for her – food, shelter and clothing. When we were living under her roof we basically went "Dutch." I had to do for myself because she refused to "take care of a grown ass man." I married her. I took her out of the Projects in the Bronx and put her into a home. She should have wanted to help me make a future for myself and for our family; but she was rebellious against everything that I was trying to do, and I grew to hate her for that.

I wanted my wife to understand the challenges of being a Black man. I knew that it was hard to be a Black woman; having the worries of being abandoned with growing children, being a sexual object for the entire world, being a single parent, being discriminated against, being hated by other races, being abused by men. I understood that and wanted to be a solution to those difficult issues that many Black women face. But I needed her to understand that as a Black man I faced all of the same issues; plus the additional issue of being considered a threat to White supremacy and dominance. Black men are a symbol of Black strength and for that reason alone – I was a target for assassination.

I needed her to understand my value and cherish my presence because at any given moment I could be killed; by another Black man that has been psychologically destroyed by this system of oppression and take out his frustration on me. I can be murdered by police for being Black and male; I can be imprisoned; as "Black" has become a substitute word for "criminal."

I never knew when one day my life would be snatched away and I wanted some type of enjoyment out of it. All these things were irrelevant to her and that bothered me immensely.

I felt alone, taken for granted; abused and deserted – even when we were together.

I believed that we could do better; that is why I never totally gave up. I never thought she would behave that way especially after I made so many sacrifices. The more I thought about it – the more I hated her. I could not escape the thoughts and bad memories that dominated my mind and I could not live with the fact that she betrayed me.

Since I could not escape – she would not escape either. I could just imagine her smiling her evil smile; knowing I was suffering and thinking "I showed him." That burned me up inside; having her think that she got the better of me after all the shit I tolerated from her. I gave her more than enough time to get right with me or let me see my children; she did not, and now my mind was made up about how to resolve the situation.

I parked my car two blocks away from where they lived with my children, my family. I walked the two blocks and waited by the side of the house. I could hear them moving around inside. She was yelling at my daughter to stop running around and for Lil Man to hurry up. They were getting ready to leave. My nerves were getting jumpy. When I heard the door open I waited, when the screen door flew open I ran as fast I could and was in front of her before she took that first step out. Her eyes bulged with fear but before she could scream like she wanted to I slapped her so hard that she fell to the floor. That's when I saw them- my babies. I almost smiled until he appeared. "Get the fuck down" I told him with clenched teeth. He was big for nothing because when I flashed that steal he immediately got down on one knee.

"All the way down" he laid on his stomach with his hands spread. "Daddy!" my daughter yelled. I told Lil Man to take the kids in the room and close the door. He had a look of fear on his face but he did what I told him to do. "Stay in there until I come and get you- you hear me?" "Yes" when I heard the door shut- I shot him. He lay there now with his life oozing out of him. She screamed I said "shut the fuck up". I rushed towards her, she tried to back away while sitting on the floor facing me crying. I did not feel for her tears. "All you had to do was let me see my kids. But no you wanted this." I mashed the gun in her face hard, it went off

Blaw! I stood over her and shot three more times then ran out of that house.

I sat at my computer and listened to a song on repeat called "Well Done" by Deitrick Haddon as I wrote a letter.

To my children,

I need you to understand that this is not what your father is nor what I was meant to be. I am sorry that I was not the best father when I had you in my life. I loved you more than words can say because you loved me for just being me. Your love for me has not yet been tainted by the harsh experiences in life that were sure to come. You were what none of my other family members were, you were mine and that would be forever. What I have done today will devastate you for the rest of your lives, and for that I feel like a coward. I know that I should have had discipline and just walked away, but something took over me and I could not rest. I became a woman beater which is wrong. I have my reasons but no excuse, only explanation I can give you is that I was out of control over my own emotions and didn't really see what it was that I was doing. I really and truly lost it.

I was supposed to be a better man a stronger man, but I was not. This is not what being a man is all about. This is not the proper manner to do things. Do not be like me. Be better than me; use me as an example of what not to do. Life is going to be hard and the people you love might not necessarily love you back and you will experience pain. Let that pain make you stronger to be able to appreciate the person that will come into your life and love you the way you deserve to be loved. I know that you will be traumatized by losing both of your parents this way. I tried to ignore it, get over it- but I could not. I am a selfish bastard and I deserve hell fire. I do not feel an ounce of remorse for her though. I just know that when I do reach hell, she will already be there.

You have to look out for each other now. Do not ever let anyone or anything come between you. You are the only family that you have. Protect one another. I pray that some day when you are older that you will somehow forgive me. I love you more than this life. With that said- I just pray that God has mercy on my soul. Goodbye my babies. Your father – Blaw!!!

The End.

Love is a powerful force, it can be beautiful or it can be grotesque, it can empower you or – destroy you. Be careful about who you fall in love with.

Confessions

Summation

Conflict Habitual Relationships

> *These relationships are characterized by an over abundance of conflictual passion, tension, discord and compulsion. Although incompatibility is apparent and pervasive; couples attempt to preserve the relationship. These couples seem to use conflict as a means of expressing their attachment to one another. – Source Unknown*

There is an inadequate amount of services for family counseling. It is also very expensive for married couples living in low-income communities. In many cities around the U.S. it is very difficult to get assistance for dysfunctional relationships and marriages; especially for the working poor and low-income households. Forcing couples to deal with problems themselves; which in many cases – is impossible to do. There should be government funding for marriage counseling that is assessable to the general public. There should be a place that couples can go or call before tragedy strikes. As a nation we know that domestic abuse is a national problem. We need to get to the root of the problem, develop solutions and give both partners an outlet to express themselves and their grievances in a productive and healthy manner. We need A National Intervention.

www.ingramcontent.com/pod-product-compliance
Lightning Source LLC
Chambersburg PA
CBHW070459030726
47503CB00004B/1108